Marquel

OTHER WORKS BY EMILY W. SKINNER

Novels by Emily W. Skinner

Marquel

Marquel's Dilemma

Marquel's Redemption

Booktrailer:
Marquel book trailer on YouTube—
featuring actor Eric Roberts & Marquel Skinner
www.youtube.com/watch?v=6e6O7iYqeVQ

Young Adult Novels by E. W. Skinner

St. Blair: Children of the Night

St. Blair: Sybille's Reign

St Blair: The Diary of St. Blair

Marquel

BY EMILY W. SKINNER

For Mom, who raised us on *Rona Barrett's Hollywood* and *Silver Screen*. I'll always remember shopping on Friday for new magazines at the newsstand.
Thank you for being you!

Check out the *Marquel* book trailer on YouTube—
featuring actor Eric Roberts & Marquel Skinner
www.youtube.com/watch?v=6e6O7iYqeVQ

ACKNOWLEGEMENTS

B egin with the end in mind.
I began writing *Marquel* shortly after the death of my mentor, Harry Whittington. Harry was one of the masters of the earliest mass-market paperback originals. The pulps. I interviewed Harry at his home on Indian Rocks Beach in Florida while I was writing features for a local beach newspaper. An author of more than 250 novels under many different names, Harry wrote westerns,  romance, movie scripts, mysteries and took over the *Mandingo* series for many years.

I kept in touch with Harry off and on throughout the years. In 1989, Harry and I connected again, when he was very ill and struggling to complete a Hawaiian novel. I attempted to be of assistance and began what was the most impressive experience of my writing life. Harry taught me how to plot, how to write a novel in a chapter-by-chapter fast pace, how to reach the characters and how to *let them* play out their story. I wasn't much help to him, but I learned. Harry asked me about my own writing and it was then I shared with him my idea for *Marquel*. Harry told me I had to outline it first, then write a sample chapter and he'd look over it. I did.

Harry wasn't one to criticize; rather, he instructed. He approved my story on his first reading of the outline and sample chapter!

"It has all the elements of a good novel," he said. He approved!

On his deathbed, he encouraged me to finish writing the novel.

With much love, I want to thank Harry Whittington for allowing me to get close enough to observe a master and to have his approval. To his widow, Kathryn Whittington, who has since passed, I appreciated her encouragement and the interest she showed in one who admired Harry and his work.

There are many people who nurture you through life and assist in making you who you are. My mother, Barbara, is one of the most important people in my life. Without her love and caring and always being home for us kids, I know I wouldn't be the person I am today. Her spirituality and sensitivity give me the foundation and hope to follow my heart. I want to thank my Dad, too. Dad and Mom divorced when I was a teen. I love them both. We are very close. To my older brother, John, my best friend in 8th grade and a great Navy man, and my younger brother, Mark, a computer guru and a modern Good Samaritan, I want to say thank you both for being in my life. To Ellen Williams, my baby sister, my best friend, and a great writer with 2 novels under her belt, I want to say thank you for being the most honest human being alive and for not giving in like so many of us do. (We should form a writer's pact!) Ellen made it possible for this book to finally get published.

Lastly, to my husband, Tom, the best husband and father, and our daughters, Marquel and Blair, who make my life complete, I want to say I love you deeply. I had predicted at 15 that I was going to have a daughter named Marquel someday and write a book by the same name. The name was the only similarity to the character Marquel when it was first published in 2001; my daughter Marquel was 15. However, my daughter, Marquel, is now an actress.

For Blair, our youngest daughter, I wrote the St. Blair series, a fictional trilogy for young adults. My daughter Blair is a young filmmaker working in Hollywood.

To God, to whom I owe my existence, thanks for making this earthly journey such an awesome experience.

PROLOGUE

"I can't get the head out! Jesus Christ...Get downstairs and get some help!"

The husband turned numbly toward the door, his eyes wet. Just a few steps away his wife had given birth to the legs and torso of his daughter. He turned to the nurse midwife. "You're going to kill her! Stop pulling...damn you...you'll rip her arms out!"

"You want brain damage? *Move. Now!*" the midwife commanded.

"It hu...hur...hurts," Joanne moaned.

"I know, sweetie. We're almost there."

Brunette clumps clung to Joanne's neck; her damp gown stuck to her swollen breasts and belly. It was 100 degrees in the small room; she was certain of it. Surely she was going to die of asphyxiation. "I..." she gripped the sides of the bed and cried out again. *God, dear God...Let this baby live...We've come...too far...Don't...take her...*Another violent pain coursed through her. Every cell, every tissue seemed to unravel. Shaking uncontrollably against the pressure, no more sound escaped her; all was strangled by the brutal force tearing her in half.

Her husband, now a sobbing heap on the hallway floor, cried and prayed. She could hear someone mounting the staircase, bounding upward. The sound was a faint pounding in her head...Or was it the blood pumping through her resounding in her eardrums?

Another nurse midwife entered.

"It's going to be okay," she assured Joanne.

The midwife hoped it would be, as she'd never seen anything quite like it. The small, rubbery figure was clamped at the head by the very canal that gave her life. "I'll take over."

She checked Joanne, noting the widening tear. The head would come, *should* come. "Just a little more, sweetie…" *Please, just a little more.*

How many hours had it been? Joanne wondered. It seemed like just moments ago her husband had been massaging her back. They were laughing. Holding hands. He had watched highlights of a football game on the small black and white television on the corner dresser as the contractions got closer. Joanne turned her focus to the wallpaper's faded red, yellow and blue flowers. Now only red, yellow and blue dots blurred beyond the slits of her heavy eyelids. The print bedspread was tossed aside, everything readied for this birth.

The nurse midwives had been very official about everything. They explained that the baby was in a breech position and the doctors at a nearby hospital could turn the baby or do a c-section. Joanne could leave and deliver there. But she was too scared. What if something happened on the way? She hadn't considered what could happen if she stayed…

The county birthing center seemed safe and homey, even if it was unusually busy. The waiting area was stacked with laboring women, each vying for one of the three available rooms. Only those in the most advanced stages of labor were admitted. The whole procedure was only to take a matter of six to eight hours according to their coach. Each family was given instructions on timing contractions, allowing the center a turnover of assembly line accuracy.

Conception had been a miracle. Tests, the only ones they could afford, never detected a problem. Instead they were told to relax, taught how to calculate ovulation, and for Joanne to keep her feet elevated after sex. Finally, they had decided she had damaged her reproductive organs during childhood—something as simple as falling off a bicycle. His sperm count was fine. She was the one at fault, the one with the problem. After seven years of trying, they gave up.

Now in year eight, they were spending a misty September morning in an old house converted into a birthing center. Behind the buttercup exterior which expelled the rich aroma of fresh brewed coffee and scrambled eggs, three lives were being torn apart. Joanne feared their bond, their commonality of a love expressed in the creation of flesh and blood, could be short-lived.

Most couples were pampered and fed once their baby arrived. Would they be the rare tragedy the center hushed up? Would they pack up and go home as they had come? Childless...

Joanne inhaled deeply. With what effort she could, she pushed.

"Good girl...Keep it up."

The first midwife returned with an oxygen tank. She assured Joanne her husband was being attended to in the kitchen downstairs.

"I...can't...do it...hurts..."

"Come on, honey. Come on."

Joanne wept.

"Focus Joanne. Do you hear me?"

"I..."

"Oh-my-God. You're there."

Joanne felt a rush of encouragement. She pushed harder. It seemed as if her heart were connected to the umbilical cord. She felt faint. Perhaps she'd die. Could her heart fall out? She shook violently. It seemed beyond her control and then it happened. The pressure stopped. The midwives looked at one another.

"Bag the baby."

Joanne wondered if the baby was dead.

The first midwife suctioned the baby's nose and mouth and then placed the oxygen mask over the infant's small face as the second midwife severed the umbilical cord. Joanne turned to see her purplish-blue child, a limp mass on the changing table.

"Bag the...? Is she...?"

The silence lasted far too long.

"She's responding. Sorry, bag is a term for oxygen."

"Thank God, oh...thank God." Joanne tried to pull herself up on her elbows.

"We'll have an ambulance take you both to the hospital. I'll get Dad."

The second midwife patted Joanne's thigh. "Push out the placenta."

"Do you think...she's suffered brain damage?"

"It's hard to say."

A greater pain mounted. Joanne closed her eyes. How could she do this again? She felt the pressure inside her growing in volume. "O-o-o-h!" She pushed until the slimy blob released itself.

"It's over. You've done a hell of a job, Mom."

Joanne smiled. She was a mother, wasn't she? She felt a well of emotion. Her baby was no longer a part of her. They were independent, yet still dependent on one another.

"You want to hold her?"

Joanne nodded. She couldn't speak, her upper lip quivering.

"Your pediatrician will answer all your questions at the hospital. She's tough, your little one." She rubbed the baby's right foot. "What's her name?"

This didn't seem real.

"Marquel." Joanne smiled at her daughter. *Her daughter.*

"How beautiful. Is it a family name?"

"No, it's...Well, we wanted our..."

"Our child to have a special name." Her husband finished the sentence for her from the open doorway.

CHAPTER ONE

1991

The evening sky, streaked gray across periwinkle, appeared as welcoming as a damp mascara-stained pillow. For eight o'clock on a Thursday evening, LA traffic wasn't bad. In fact, at this hour, traffic usually moved in and out of the city without incident. All sound was sealed out by the hum of the air conditioner and the car radio. Familiar were the streams of headlights and streetlights cutting through the closing darkness, casting their luminous beams upon the city of angels.

Marquel reached into the gray vinyl console and retrieved a Lucite box. *The Joshua Tree*, U2. Popping the cassette into the Blaupunkt, she sat upright and squared her shoulders, then punched the turbo to the limit.

It was a high, driving to the right music.

A slight thrust rocked her hips as the Saab moved fluidly under her. It was new, gunmetal gray with a slash of silver pinstriping. Its dove velour interior was bathed in her scent, a mixture of Tabu and perm solution.

I STILL HAVEN'T FOUND WHAT I'M LOOKING FOR...

"How true," she mumbled. Her white-blonde locks were Shirley Temple bouncy, all but a straight sweep of bangs brushed slightly askew. Thank God the idiot got it right this time! How many times had she told him to let the solution set longer? She knew her hair better than he did. Not a strand of natural curl existed in her camouflaged roots.

Honking at a tour bus, she made a wide sweep around the vehicle and shook her fist at the driver. Why the hell did he drive so slowly? She *had* to go faster.

She glanced in the rear-view mirror; wide-set violet eyes assessed the crimson lipstick covering the full, collagen-injected lips. Ken said her mouth didn't have the pouty appeal the directors had become so found of, so she had the job done. Ken advanced her the money on her first commercial and there it was, the pout. She ran a finger through the V of her upper lip.

Cheap lipstick.

Why did she steal the crap? For some reason, she'd found herself in a drug store with a pocket full of Maybelline cosmetics—when for Christ's sake she just signed a $100,000 per episode contract!

It didn't tickle Ken.

Her agent had literally put her life in order, housing her in his lover's Malibu home for more than six months. Evan was less anal, the strong one in the relationship. Ken was the panicky, overburdened partner who wanted control, yet couldn't maintain it. Evan was the glue who held his high-strung lover together and kept him in check. Marquel wondered what she or Ken would do if Evan ever kicked them out.

Richard Guy of GuyRex, the beauty contestant gurus, couldn't have done a better job polishing Marquel's appearance. She laughed bitterly. An up-and-comercoming shoplifting in a friggin' K-Mart. What the hell was wrong with her? She shut the air conditioner off and carefully slid back the sunroof. The damn thing had caused the loss of more than one manicure.

The release of pressure pushed her tassel-fine blondeness down, sending tendrils dancing upward and outward. She slid the sleeves of her Calvin Klein cashmere up to the elbow, freeing her arms, and shifted gears. She could smell it now. A gust of humid air brought the perm solution to life.

Great! It smelled like a cat pissed on her head.

She glanced in the side-view mirror and caught a glimpse of color. Then she looked into her rear-view mirror and saw him.

California Highway Patrol.

Erik Estrada she could do without. She swung across two lanes and slowed the car to a stop, waiting for the patrolman to dismount and make his approach.

Shit! It suddenly hit her. Her heart began to pound. She tapped the steering wheel and looked straight ahead. What was it Ken said? *Keep out of trouble.* She smiled. Then she remembered that Ken and Evan had taken off for a long weekend. This was her chance to drown in a bottle of their fine wine and soak in the hot tub for a few days. "Can't do this..." she felt an odd surge of emotion. She ejected the tape and rolled the window down.

"Is there a problem, officer?" her voice quavered. She kept her watering eyes focused on the hood of the car.

"Are you aware of how fast you were going?"

"Well, no," she lied. *He* wasn't going to do this to her. She felt her nose begin to run and brushed her hand over it. "I suppose I got impatient...drove a little faster than usual." *God, how could she let this motorcycle cowboy affect her this way?*

He asked for her driver's license. Her palms were now damp. She reached into her bag for the Gucci wallet and retrieved the license, her hands trembling. *Stop.* She felt certain she was going to lose it, cry out loud. *Focus, focus.* Crossing her arms, she leaned out the window and watched him scribble something. Her arms felt heavy, like warm clay melting over the window's rubber molding. *Don't pass out.* She started to yawn over and over.

She looked familiar. The name on the license hit him. "You're Marquel. *Suburban Life*, right?"

The press was prying, everyone was. The damn press had had a heyday already. Ken was pissed that she didn't read the trades or watch television. She *was* television, why watch it? Why should she care what others think? She preferred to keep an invisible persona in her own mind. She couldn't take all this seriously.

Yet, what could she take seriously? At times she longed for the solitude and beauty of Thoreau's *Walden*. But these thoughts depressed her. *Stop, damn it. Focus.* Driving to the right music gave her strength and power…She blurted out a loud laugh.

"Ma'am?"

She didn't feel as lightheaded now. "I'm the one. The one and only." She gave him a wide grin. "You want to stop by the set Monday? I could get you in." *Say no…*

He handed her the ticket. "No. But it'll be my pleasure to add your name to my roster of celebrity violators."

"The pleasure's all mine. What kind of music do you drive to?"

"My dispatcher is all the music I need." He wasn't returning the smile.

"Guess when you have the right speed you're driving to a good tune."

"Ma'am, let's not head down this path…"

"I have but one path by which my feet are guided and that is the lamp of experience! Or some crap like that. Do you know who said that?"

He didn't respond. He wasn't amused by her. He gritted his teeth. She was beginning to sound like a smartass.

"Patrick Henry," she offered finally.

"He also said, 'Give me liberty or give me death.' Don't hurt yourself or anyone else in your pursuit of liberty."

"Good point. Well taken."

"Drive safely."

"Yes, sir," she saluted, then quickly regretted it. She could tell she was one step from   form of corrective action or, God forbid, being pulled physically from her car. She closed her eyes and began mentally counting, hoping he would leave.

Was she going to cry? He stared at her.

She could feel his eyes boring through her. "I'm praying," she said. *Praying you'll leave.* "I'll be moving on in a minute."

He didn't respond. Just shook his head and went back to his motorcycle. She seemed strange, but not under the influence. He'd keep his distance and follow her awhile to make certain.

"That's all it took," she told *People* magazine. "I did *My Fair Lady* at the Burt Reynolds Theater and later did some work at MGM in Orlando."

"Anyway, my first part, in *My Fair Lady* was insignificant…A critic wrote that I looked like the saddest street person he'd ever seen." She pouted, then paused to inhale a drag of the thin brown cigarette resting between two perfectly lacquered nails. Laughing, she tossed her head back, pitching platinum curls over one shoulder to reveal the now-famous violet eyes. "One thing led to another," she continued. "Guess I'd never have made it out of the boonies if not…"

Rehearsed. The story had been repeated more than twenty times at the media junket. *Suburban Life,* a contemporary drama series, was the network's trump card in the fall lineup. Her role as Sharon had already secured an Emmy nomination.

"Who would've guessed I'd have a series of my own? I'm a stage actress," she looked past the magazine writer to the next eager reporter. Impatiently she crushed out the cigarette in an amber glass ashtray and called out, "Next."

Marquel. A single name celebrity soon to join the ranks of Cher, Madonna and Bono.

Zach Manning twisted a charcoal thread dangling from the belt loop of his Brooks Brothers trousers. The woman on the couch was repeating herself. She was annoying and gassy. Had he heard a word?

He didn't need to; the story never changed. She had convinced herself her husband was impotent—theirs was a sexless marriage. Should she take a lover? Would making him jealous work? Her body turned him off—she used to have a cute ass.

If only he could say what she really needed to hear without sending her over the edge. *Divorce the bastard, stop eating burritos and get a job! No one cares if you're trying to save the planet by not eating meat. You are a self-polluting, self-absorbed hunk of flesh that would make a great meal for some poor starving mountain lion. Sacrifice yourself to those deprived meat-eating animals you want so desperately to preserve...*

No, she wanted to save the marriage, despite the fact her husband was getting his elsewhere. Therapy would make things right again. She'd find the wrong and make it right. Right for *him*.

What sense did Hollywood make? The place was crawling with insecure assholes earning enough to bail out the federal deficit twice. Christ, he wanted to get back to some grass roots. Maybe talk to Sheen. The actor seemed to be getting away from the glitz and back to real issues. He'd make a note to call Martin on Monday.

Why, in God's name, had he opened a practice in Beverly Hills? *Isabel.*

She'd insisted they move to California just after the wedding. She wanted to be close to her girlfriends, drive fancy cars and dine with the stars. They'd done it all. And now, twenty years later, they were divorced and shared only a single common interest, their 14-year-old daughter Jackie.

Both were civil about the arrangement. He paid a healthy chunk of alimony and child support; Isabel kept the house, the kid, the Bentley and the maid. He moved to Century City and got Jackie on weekends; she shopped, played tennis and did lunch.

Nothing ever changed.

His patients never seemed to change either. The starlet screwed the star, director, producer...anyone for a part. No, the women's movement didn't change Hollywood. Everyone still did each other to get ahead. Some got more head than others. The director screamed when the little cunt fell in love with him, 'cause dammit, he didn't need that shit. He had a wife, after all, a good marriage.

Good marriage?

And the wives, the ones who weren't screwing around, didn't know why their husbands weren't interested.

Was it his age? Her sagging tits? Well?

What a mystery, he signed. He pulled the gray thread, curled it up with his thumb and index finger and tossed it on the marble top coffee table. "Mrs. Porter, we're out of time. Let's pick up Tuesday with that last thought." He nodded reassurance.

When the woman disappeared, he took her place on the warm leather couch. Running the fingers of both hands through his straight black peppered tresses, he stretched his neck, moving the taut muscles from side to side. His hair characteristically stood up in a cropped fashion, the effect of a crew-cut grown out. Closing olive-complected lids, he rested his tired black eyes. At 52, he knew there had to be more to this stinking life than work and golf.

He had Jackie. But Jackie only filled part of the void. She was a good kid. Never got into trouble. Didn't smoke or drink that he knew of. Maybe he needed to move out of the high-rise and into a house. A place where she could spread out. Even if it was only for the weekend.

Ken Avery answered the intercom. "What is it? I'm long distance with New York…"

The angel-voice whispered, "He says he's with *Pursuit*. He wants an interview with Marquel. Should he hold?" She sounded as if she were out of breath.

Ken rolled his aquamarine eyes. This one was brilliant at screening calls. "If he'll hold indefinitely."

"Okay, Ken…uh, Mr. Avery."

Bimbo. All secretaries were nothing but plastic-faced bimbos. Maybe he should get a guy to sit out there and field calls.

"This is Avery." He punched the speaker on the flashing button with his pencil. "Make it quick, I'm on the other line." He toyed with the pencil, then leaned over and began rummaging through his desk drawers.

"Mark Collins with *Pursuit*. I'd like to interview Marquel on the set of *Suburban Life*."

"What'd you say your name was?"

"Collins."

"As in Tom Collins?"

"The son of."

Ken felt satisfaction as he retrieved a Cross pen he'd feared he'd lost. "The son of?"

"Do I have an interview?"

"No."

"Ken, work with me here."

"Whatever your name is, the answer is no. We don't do tab trash."

"We're weekly trash. Keeps your client's name in front of the public. Millions of TV viewers read us for their star fix. What's so bad about a little trash?"

"It rots, smells and needs to be disposed of."

"Before it rots it's consumable, digestible and you have the option of recycling."

"You're not selling me, Collins. Flying dogs on the set of *Suburban Life*. Marquel held captive by alien Elvis clone. You don't need my client to write that crap." Ken punched the button disconnecting the man.

He checked the other line. The tinkling music box chimed "It's a Small World." Dammit, would they ever pick up?

"Mr. Avery?" Angel-voice interrupted. "Mr. Collins says he was accidentally disconnected."

This jerk had balls. "It was no accident."

"He's real polite, should I ask…"

"To hold? *Je*-sus! Listen, no more calls today. I'm out, got it?"

"Yes, but what about…"

He punched the flashing button. "Collins you're pissing me off!"

"The feeling is mutual."

"Sell me."

"I'm trying. What can I say? You hate tabloids, I write for one."

"And?"

"And I can put your client on the cover every week for a month with just an hour on the set. You and I know the trailer park crowd and low- to middle-income families consume most of the junk food *Suburban Life's* sponsors promote. They're also the same folks who read our magazine. Even bad supermarket press usually reaps a sympathy response. 'That poor girl doesn't need those press people prying into her life.' Ken, it's a win/win situation. No one with a brain takes us seriously. Though, personally, I like to have an element of truth to a story."

"So you admit you make it up. And now I'm just another of those folks without a brain."

"I don't. No, you're not."

"Like I'm supposed to feel warm and fuzzy now."

"No, cold and indifferent will work. Do I have the interview or not?"

"You're good. You're a liar, but good. You want a job? I've got screenwriters who can't pitch worth a damn. They can write their asses off, but get them in front of key people and they fall apart."

"Ken, I'm flattered."

"The answer is still no."

"Let's pretend I work for the *Times* or *Chronicle*…"

"And?"

"Sixty minutes on the set. What harm can come from it?"

Ken sighed. "I'm gonna take a chance here. Call tomorrow for a day and time."

"Thank you…"

"You only get one chance, Collins. Don't fuck it up."

Ken punched the flashing button, disconnecting Collins. "Yes, I'll hold." He broke the pencil in half. Who the hell did they think they were talking to? He punched the intercom, "Terry."

Angel voice. "Yes, Mr. Avery?"

"You sit on this line. When they pick up, for God's sake sound professional, then connect me."

"Yes sir."

Yes sir. Was he her friggin' father now?

CHAPTER TWO

"Mind keeping your foot off my desk?" John Gilman grabbed the younger man's shoe and pushed it to the floor. Walking behind the desk he plopped his wide, bus driver's ass on the high-backed leather chair.

"Calm down…I've got the hottest story since the Menendez murders." The blond man leaned in, both palms flat on the desktop. "Avery's giving me tomorrow on the set. I can dig up enough on this mysterious soap slut to keep *Pursuit* covers filled for the next month."

"You're a cocky bastard, Collins. What makes you think there's a story?"

"It's a gut feeling." Collins observed his boss's mid-section.

The man was disgusting. Collins would never let himself get in such a pathetic state. While Gilman was responsible for hiring him, Collins couldn't help feeling sick any time he had to spend more than 10 minutes with the man. Gilman reeked of body odor. His breath—a blend of coffee, cigarettes and God knew what else—had the fragrance of a dump downwind. Uniformed in wide-band polyester pants and a cotton button-down shirt with brown underarm stains, Gilman was once a brilliant mind. His career in the dailies had been cutting edge. He broke more news and appeared at more New York functions than any one of the great gossip columnists. He knew who was doing whom and why. He knew what to run and what to withhold. His downfall came when his addictions made him incapable of writing. Unable to concentrate or communicate in a rational manner, Gilman soon lost the trust of the prominent. His comeback in the tabloids was without fanfare. Journalists knew his byline, but he was old and passé by 40. Now in his late 60s, Gilman was Jabba the Hut but still sharp when it came to smoking out a good story.

"You listenin' to me, boy?" Gilman swayed in the leather chair and laughed softly. The editor had seen dubious reporters come and go, but at last he'd met one who understood the essence of a good lead. He didn't dare give the younger man too much credit; the young reporter wasn't ready. He could tell Collins had little regard for his experience and he could care less. He studied the 20-year-old. His starbursted brown irises transfixed on the younger's cold blues. "Collins...son of a bitch, you gonna get me something good?"

Collins grinned.

"I'm glad you showed up tonight...just came from a stakeout in Vegas. Seems we have a recently divorced congressman marrying a 17-and-a-half-year-old Ford model. Doesn't look good..." The older man shook his head, pausing as he always did for emphasis. "Her Momma was standing right behind him with her red-hot wallet shoved up his ass."

"No kidding." Collins impatiently rested either elbow on his far spread knees. "Melody Mars marrying that doe-eyed Kansas farmhand. What the hell's going on?"

"Who knows? I think she's knocked up..." The older man pointed to a framed *Pursuit* cover. The issue featured the model clad in nothing but a teddy, escorted by yet another prominent figure, the son of a former United States president. "And since Momma won't be getting her monthly take from Melody, she's making sure Poppa Politician feeds her some of *his* kickbacks."

"Right on, Mom. I'll be Eileen's pissed."

"Listen, Paulina she isn't. Eileen has better...now Kansas will finally see the return of Toto."

"Low blow."

"'Cause I don't like the woman from Mars?" Gilman wheezed. His large basketball-belted gut shook. "Get something for next week's header…following Melody's nuptials, we're riding your Marquel wave awhile." He laced the fingers of both hands together, placing them behind his head to reveal damp ringed underarms as stronger body odor filled the close space. "What's your angle?"

"My guess is she's hooked on snow."

"Who hasn't been?"

"She'll end up in Betty Ford soon. Can't run a high-rated soap with the star on hiatus."

"What about men…who's she running with?"

"Not certain. She's under wraps. Not much of a hobnobber."

"Maybe she likes girls?"

"I don't think so."

"I thought you had something? Damn it, don't waste my time on a small coke story."

"She's been jilted by a married guy. Someone in power," he lied. The old man was really pissing him off.

"We've got that. A Melody in reverse I don't need. I want something that smells…"

"Manufactured or otherwise?"

"The truth. If this lady has something to hide, her story's gotta be better than anything we can come up with."

"Agreed." Collins sat up in the narrow vinyl chair. Gilman grinned at him through yellow crooked teeth. The fat bastard looked as evil as a bloated Jack Nicholson. Someday the stupid fucker would be out on the street. Surely he couldn't last much longer in his cholesterol-clogged condition.

Christ! Why hadn't the tab been turned into a TV show? After all, *Pursuit* was bigger than any Murdoch product to date.

Collins left Gilman's office and headed toward his cubicle. He wanted to rise fast. No years of toil like his father. No hoping. He was going to see to it he was a success. His father, Tom, had been a life insurance salesman in a small community in northern

California. He couldn't sell worth a damn; he didn't understand relationship selling. He'd been schooled by a manager who told him to "shut up" after the pitch. He lived and died by the "last word" rule. The next person to speak was to be the buyer, *with* an affirmative answer. So Tom would sit and stare at his prospects for as long as it took—to either be thrown out or intimidate the individual into buying. Once word got around about the Tom Collins' technique, people would invite him into their home and bust a gut when he'd shut up. Tom had been left in more than one parlor. Proud of his training, Tom shared with anyone who would listen the process of shutting up after a presentation. It didn't take long for news to travel from the diner to the business community to the residents that this man had a problem. Certainly his wardrobe, his scraggly son Mark, and his wife Lila's work as a maid revealed the level of his success.

Tom tinkered with television and radio repair in his spare time and could have made a good living in that profession if he'd opened a small shop. His father couldn't afford to buy Mark more than a couple pairs of pants and shirts each school season. So Mark wore the clothes his mother made him in elementary school and stole from department stores once he reached junior high. He lied and told his parents that his friends were giving him clothes they'd outgrown. He secretly suspected that they knew what he was doing, but didn't want to confront the situation. After all, what honor was there in admitting that you couldn't clothe your kid like everyone else? Tom would then have to quit sales and get a real job.

Tom died when Mark graduated high school. Mark had just picked up his diploma and waved it high when he glanced out to see if his parents were watching. Lila was on her feet viewing him through the Instamatic. At the time the flash went off, he noticed the old man wasn't moving, not even looking up. His father appeared to be taking a nap, yet Mark knew the noise in the auditorium was far too loud for that. Tom had died during the ceremony. Mark would never know if Tom had heard his name being called or if his dad had seen him pick up the diploma. Lila's photos of that moment still haunt him. Mark's expression is painfully void. He wanted to believe his father left this earthly world through the flash of the camera, following the light on to the next dimension.

Life without Tom was better for both Mark and Lila. His mother quickly remarried. Mark's stepfather Bob was a local banker and he generously paid Mark's way through college. Lila never worked for another day as a housekeeper. Instead, she found happiness with a handsome, wealthy country club man. It was so much easier when Bob was in charge. Mark later found out that Lila had been cleaning Bob Masterson's house for two years prior to becoming Mrs. Masterson. Mark didn't know if they had been having an affair or if the man had simply fallen in love with his cleaning woman. Mark couldn't imagine his mother cheating on his father, yet wouldn't blame her if she did. He never asked.

Mark devoured college. He loved the lifestyle, learning and freedom. He finished after 36 months of non-stop study. He wanted to use his education to move forward and he wasn't picky about who his new employer would be. His mass communications degree gave him a multitude of options, but writing was the one skill he desired to hone and utilize above all else. So when Gilman called him back after the second interview, he gladly accepted.

He grabbed a pad and began making notes for the Marquel interview. He had landed the most important interview of his new career and he needed to be prepared. He smiled, thinking about Ken Avery's remarks. The guy sounded like a real wimp. He wouldn't have given *himself* the time of day, so he couldn't figure out why Avery granted the interview. It didn't matter.

Leaning over the caterer's tray of crab-stuffed mushrooms, Isabel Manning moaned in orgasmic approval. Dinner parties were her trademark. Her gastronomic events featured only a few guests, real conversationalists, and the best variety of designer foods.

She prided herself on the forced bohemian flair. It was a calling of sorts. She was appreciated most for her up-and-comings, the sculptors, new comics and writers. And this dinner party would certainly seal her obligations for the following month.

Dear Sophie.

She smiled wickedly at the thought of her oldest and dearest friend bringing a new date. What was his name? She snapped her fingers to jog her memory. Sam. Sam something. A beefcake on one of the new soaps.

This could prove interesting. She licked her lips.

Of course, Lyle would be by her side tonight. Popping a plump mushroom into her mouth, she cupped a palm under her chin, then dabbed her thin lips with a linen napkin and checked the next aluminum tray of duck sausage.

Lyle was an interesting man, unlike Zach. Her ex-husband refused to socialize. Lyle Herlbert was a Hollywood entertainment attorney up to his neck in power. And he liked to talk.

So *interesting*. She moved down the counter, inhaling the fragrance of the blood-red roses Lyle had sent earlier. Humming, she turned to the sink and ran her hands under the tap. Patting them dry on a dish towel, she perked her ears.

The phone trilled in the distance. She heard Carmen mumble, putting the caller on hold. Smoothing her palms over her severe ash brown chignon, Isabel waited for the maid to appear. She disinterestedly straightened the sterling turquoise belt hugging her hips.

"Eez Meester Zak," the Mexican woman said.

"Thank you, Carmen. If you would finish up and change, please..."

The dark woman smiled.

Isabel picked up the kitchen phone and removed a silver nugget earring. "Where the hell have you been? You were supposed to be here at noon." She exhaled. "I've asked Jackie to wait in her room. You know how much she enjoys pestering me when I'm having guests."

"Perhaps if you allowed her to meet them she wouldn't be so curious," Zach answered. "Really, telling her to hide?"

"She's watching those damn videos…and what difference does it make? Her hormones and mine are on a collision course every day it seems. I'd appreciate a little more understanding, thank you."

"Izzy, menopause doesn't become you."

"Funny. You know damn well I'm nowhere near menopause."

"Keep trying to convince yourself, honey. It's good you're optimistic. Would you like Jackie to meet me a block from the house? Or say, loitering outside the gate?"

"Fuck you."

"Would you like a raincheck…?" He laughed in a low baritone. "See you in twenty minutes."

"Make it ten." She thrust the receiver at the wall and exited the kitchen.

"Jackie! Don't ignore me…your father's on his way. Get down here this *minute*!" She took the stairs two at a time. "I'm not talking to hear myself. I expect an answer." She mounted the top landing and lurched for the first door on her right. "Do you hear me?"

The room was empty. A small television played loudly to four rock-postered walls, vibrating the fish net and plastic spiders webbed across the cathedral ceiling. In the southernmost corner a pyramid of stuffed animals guarded a large Oreo® cookie bed layered in sheets of black and white.

"I can't take this!" Isabel pounded on the bathroom door. "Are you in there?" Then trying the knob, she swung the door inward. The scent of steamy lilacs filled her nostrils. The shower curtain had been drawn back, the mirror fogged, yet no Jackie in sight.

Okay…this wasn't going to upset her. Composed, she pursed her lips, then calmly left the teen's room, not bothering to turn off the television. Pulling the door closed, she walked a few steps to the landing and began her descent. As she traveled down the staircase, she could hear Carmen in high-pitched Mexican gibberish.

She picked up speed, heels clicking through the long hall and peered in the kitchen. Jackie, long damp strands of smoke-blond hair clinging to her neck, was clad in nothing but an oversized faded sweatshirt that read "Don't Worry, Be Happy."

Carmen met Isabel's gaze. The short Mexican woman bore the expression of a hurt child. She had obviously only had time to change into a fresh white slip before accosting the girl.

Jackie, dripping wet, smirked at her mother.

Isabel's eyes fell on the plate the child was carrying. Piled high with *her* catered delicacies. "What in hell are you doing?"

"I'm getting something to eat. Do you mind?"

"Yes, I mind. Carmen take the plate from her. Your father will feed you."

The maid moved toward the girl.

"Relax, Carmen. I won't fight you." The teen shoved the plate into her mother's hands. "I don't want your big dick sausage anyway."

"You aren't going to talk to me like this." Isabel thrust the plate at Carmen, who was now keeping her eyes to the floor. "Trying to test me? It isn't going to work." She grabbed Jackie's arm and squeezed it tight. "You don't do this to your father."

"Daddy doesn't have 'off limits' at his place." The girl's eyes teared.

"Fine. Go live with him."

"Really, Mother? Then what would you have over him?" She pulled from her mother's grip.

"If you want something to eat, *ask*."

"I live here, remember. Do I need permission?"

"You know damn well what I mean."

"Fine. May I have a Coke?"

"Carmen." Isabel nodded toward the refrigerator. The maid found a red and white can and handed it to the girl. "Now get dressed. Daddy will be here *soon*." Isabel ignored the girl's hurt expression and stormed out.

"Meez Jackie." Carmen held out her arms to the girl. Jackie sobbed, allowing the older woman to rock her.

Carmen was the one person Jackie could count on, other than her father. The elder woman had tried to stop her; Jackie didn't think they'd actually believe she would eat all that food. It was a joke.

Jackie returned the maid's loving hug.

"Be good for Meez Ez'abel," Carmen whispered, pulling the wet hair from the teen's neck and began smoothing out the strands with her fingers, combing them through the girl's hair.

Jackie smiled.

Carmen pointed to the words on the girl's shirt.

"The understatement of the year," Jackie sighed.

Carmen frowned.

The teen wiped the tears from her eyes. "At least Daddy loves me."

"Meez Ez'abel love you."

"Yeah, right." The girl kissed her on the cheek then pulled away, padding out of the kitchen.

CHAPTER THREE

She had been ready for the past hour. Everything was going fine; they were going to get out early...until Joyce pulled her usual tantrum.

Marquel closed her eyes, breathing in the odor of the heavy cosmetics the make-up girl applied. Today was the last straw. If the selfish bitch wanted to control the show, she'd walk. Let them figure out what to do then.

"Sid, I can't take those kids. They make me nuts," Joyce pleaded. "Can't we pretend she's in the next room?"

"If you'd put as much energy into your character as you put into these damn delays, you might win yourself an Emmy," the director scowled, punching on finger into the middle of the woman's billowing chest.

Joyce Oswald was a thorn in Sid Carnie's side. She'd managed to stall nearly every shoot with one complaint or another. Not just complaints, but full-blown fits over menial things. She was convinced everyone, including Sid, was out to get her.

They stared at her, they yawned nearby, they silently made tapping motions with their feet. Anything to make her screw up.

Or so she claimed.

Sid pulled off his Dodgers cap, scratching the bald scalp with the chewed nails of his bony fingers. Christ, his head would be bleeding before the day was over. He needed Maalox, something to stop the erupting volcano in his flat, shrunken belly. If it wasn't

Joyce screaming or Marquel in catatonic dreamland, it was Sam worrying about which way his dick was hanging.

What next?

A summer stock veteran, Joyce was known by her friends in the theater as the actress most likely to head for off-Broadway greatness, maybe even landing the lead in a potential Tony winner. Yet fate had pre-cast her in *Suburban Life*. Ty Mayo, the program's creator and noted boob man, had seen the busty actress in *Kiss Me Kate* prior to a casting call.

He wanted her.

Not only for her talent, but for her sizable 40G mammaries.

There was no doubt in Ty's mind that the short buxom brunette was enormously gifted. She could act her way in and out of a nearly any role she put her mind to. If only she could take her mind off herself long enough to get into character.

"Get your hands off me," she shrieked at Sid.

"Like it or not Joyce, the Clip twins are a major part of the show. If you don't like playing mommy, maybe we'll have you killed off."

"Killed off, ha. Do they kill off the stars of *Thirtysomething*? Get real."

"Then you could be the runaway mother. I don't give a shit... Just so long as you don't upset those kids."

The kids, a set of identical eighteen-month-old strawberry blonde cherubs, alternately played Katie, Melissa and Jack's daughter. Sarah and Emma Clip, recruits from Clio-winning baby food ads, were the kick-off promotion for the soap. Their photos had graced the cover of nearly every woman's and parent's publication the summer before the fall lineup.

Joyce's Melissa was *Suburban Life's* homemaker/sculptor, married to an aggressive and abusive penny stock hustler, Jack Newsome, played by hunk-of-the-year, Sam Kindred. Porsche-driving, highly successful, single next-door neighbor, Sharron—Marquel's role—was the drama's central character.

Sharron is fed advice from the married couples. She is their pseudo-mascot, a token of single life, the fast lane and freedom. However, they all must settle for reality, suburban life.

While Jack and Melissa struggle to make ends meet, Sharron aspires to be a model. Earning her living as a professional contestant in wet T-shirt and bikini contests, she sails through life purchasing or winning her heart's desire, while her neighbors battle it out nightly over bills.

Sharron is shallow, self-centered and concerned only with superficial attention. Her neighbors and friends, on the other hand, could care less about her body beautiful. Instead, they enjoy the funny blonde, who, when occasionally caught off guard, laughs at herself.

Did Joyce get the message? Marquel wondered. Kill her off... wouldn't that be a hoot? Then Sharron and Jack would probably get together and raise the kid. Not a bad idea.

The makeup girl applied more blush. She could almost doze if it weren't for the chaos. How often had she taken time to just relax? Close her eyes...sleep?

Sleep. The brush strokes on her cheeks and forehead made her think of cattails and pussy willows. She imagined she was lying in a field with hand outstretched, caressing her face with the fuzzy-headed plant. Why couldn't she sleep alone? Yet there was no one to sleep with. Just sleep. Sure, she'd had her share of partners, but sex didn't feel good now. There was something missing. She would have settled for sleeping with another woman, a grandmotherly type, but even women wanted more. Afraid to close her eyes at night, she found herself nervous and exhausted by sun-up. She couldn't concentrate. She shook her head.

"Is there something wrong?" The makeup girl inquired.

"I was just thinking."

"It must be very intense. You need a massage."

"Yes, I suppose I do." But she knew she had to be on her guard. She yawned. Ken had sent some columnist over to watch the shoot.

Was the guy here? Watching quietly and taking down the sordid details of the Joyce fiasco…

"Okay everyone…" Sid made a few announcements.

Things were about to roll. She opened her eyes, noticing the blonde man standing next to a wiry Sid. Collins, she guessed. He was no doubt a punk.

The makeup girl removed the towel as she stood. Marquel gave the reporter an obliging nod, which he returned with a wet-lipped grin.

A tangle of electrical cord and hovering cameras, like pre-historic dinosaurs moving in on their prey, circled the set of Melissa's kitchen. She moved through the jungle of objects to her place near a Formica counter. Sharron, her character, was having a discussion with Melissa, Joyce's character, when the action would turn to the baby, who was supposedly hurt after tumbling off a step ladder.

"Everyone in place."

A few young men scurried in with measuring tapes, straightening cookie jars and dishes. The hunched figures quickly made an assessment of the yellow appliances, breakfast nook and made off to a bell tower in the darkness. A disembodied voice called one man back. He hurried in, placing a brand name cereal box in full view.

"Action."

Joyce delivered the first lines, while Marquel concentrated on her focal point behind the actress, at the exact same spot Collins had taken behind camera two. Her eyes stayed on his shoulder, careful not to make eye contact.

Melissa was complaining about something. She responded with her four lines. A small laugh, a gurgling noise caught her ear. For a moment it was as though she had heard the sound before.

Melissa continued. Marquel delivered her next lines distractedly. A chill ran through her, but the hot lights soon warmed the sensation sending gooseflesh along her bare arms.

"Jack is so…" Melissa stopped.

"What?" Marquel questioned.

"Insensitive, he..."

A loud cry startled Marquel. She jumped, looking for the source. Katie was screaming. "Oh my God...is she hurt?" She ran beside Melissa, sobbing.

Marquel picked up the child, kissing her fat little hands. "Are you okay, honey? I am sorry, so sorry." She bounced the baby on her shoulder, placing her hand behind the baby's head, urging the child to put her head down. The baby girl held her arms out to a woman off in the darkness.

Joyce moved so it appeared the baby was calling to her.

"We won't let this happen again..." Marquel continued. The child struggled, pushing her chubby hands in Marquel's face. "It's okay," she shook the curly-haired girl up and down on her hip.

The baby let out another high-pitched scream.

Joyce tried to ad-lib, reaching for the infant. This wasn't in the script. What the hell was Marquel doing? Showboating for the blonde guy?

"Cut."

The child's mother ran into the heavily-lit kitchen, reaching for the baby whose outstretched hands were fighting their way to her. Marquel looked at the woman in amazement, holding the child tighter.

"Momma," the baby squealed. Her red little face held a steady stream of fresh tears.

"Let go of her," the woman insisted. "Marquel, you're scaring her. If you ever...forget it, you're not listening."

"I'm sorry, Katie." Marquel kissed the baby's head.

"Katie?" The mother rolled her eyes. "It's okay, Sarah."

Sid ran in, cap in his back pocket, scratching his head furiously with both hands. "What the hell just happened?"

There was mumbling among the crew. Collins stroked the cleft of his chin with his index finger, grinning like a Cheshire cat. He couldn't wait for the finale, let alone the encore.

Joyce stormed past him muttering assorted obscenities.

"Gotta minute?"

"What's it worth to ya?"

"I just have a few questions."

"Was that your idea or hers?" She was certain Marquel put him up to this.

"Idea? I'm only here to observe."

"Observe what?"

"Don't get hyper." He held both hands up. "Does she get like this often?"

"And you are?"

"Mark Collins with *Pursuit*."

"Avery?"

"Yes."

"That prick is a piss poor excuse for an agent. *Pursuit*? So now she's selling out to the tabs?"

"I gather her reaction to the kid wasn't in the script."

"Figure it out for yourself, bud." Joyce brushed her breasts against his arms, trying to get past him.

"Obviously it wasn't."

"Did you study journalism through some mail-order program or did you get a promotion from *Pursuit* janitor to reporter?"

"Does she get like this often?" he repeated, wanting to smack the bitch.

"One thing." She knew anything she told him would get blown out of proportion. No sense giving in so easily; two could play this game. She eyed the set. Sid had one arm around Marquel's waist as he walked with her. She turned back to the blonde man, giving him a sober look. "Honestly, I think she had an abortion. I was real crazy the last one I had. I almost lost it over the whole thing. It's gotta be hormonal, 'cause I'm no baby person. But Marquel...hell, babies bein' around probably makes her feel guilty...like she killed her kid or something."

"Who was the father?"

"You, for all I know."

He ignored the comment.

"She ain't one for kissin' and tellin.'"

"Is she usually this irrational?"

"Off the record, she blacks out occasionally, just stands there like a crazy person…We did an outdoor shoot once and she thought she heard a gun go off. Just froze. Stood there listening. I mean, no one, but no one, can figure this chick out."

"You think she'd talk to me?"

"Avery sent you."

"I mean in-depth."

"Not about abortion. Barbara Walters you're not. Don't go asking her about it. Besides, she doesn't do interviews. Oh, she talks like a broken record, but that's about it."

"Thanks."

"For what?"

He glanced at the set. It was now deserted. "You going to continue?"

"Go ask stick man. Of course we're continuing."

"Carnie is stick man?"

"You see any others?"

He liked her. A little too top-heavy, but cut in the right places. He wondered how she'd survived being such a big mouth. No one likes a rat. But he gathered she held her ammunition well, spitting it out only when it suited her.

Zach tapped his foot impatiently, staring through the etched glass windows in the double doors. "Come on, Carmen." He dug his hands in his trouser pockets, then glanced around at the manicured lawn. "Not bad. Glad my money sees greener pastures."

The door swung in. The maid gave him a wide, toothy grin. "Meester Zak."

He gave her a hug.

"Jackie be down in minute," Carmen moved out of his way to let him in.

"Fine. Is her mother available?"

"Meez Ez'abel change."

"That I would like to see…" He sat at the foot of the stairs, not bothering to intrude on his ex-wife's territory.

"Daddy," Jackie called from the top stair.

"Hi, punkin."

"Where are we going this weekend?"

"I thought we'd play it by ear. Or did you have something in mind?"

"I don't know."

"We can discuss it on the way. Get your bag, baby." He twisted around to see her. "Why don't we drive to the beach and have a hot dog, then take in a movie?"

"Or we could just hang out and watch TV. Maybe cruise the halls for Tom? Have you seen Mr. Selleck lately?"

"A little old for you, isn't he?"

"Daddy, I do think he's handsome and funny."

"I thought rock stars were more your speed."

"I'm flexible."

"Get moving."

"Yes sir."

"Zach," Isabel crept up behind Jackie.

"Izzy."

"I'd appreciate it if you would talk with your daughter about her smart mouth."

He stared up at the woman atop the stairs. Dressed from head to toe in white cotton knit, she looked fabulous. Designer something, he guessed. He couldn't keep labels straight. Large padded shoulders diverted from the swell of her breasts giving her loosely-belted, bejeweled waistline a leek, svelte appearance. Ornate baubles in emerald and gold tones matching both the stones in her belt and sandals, draped in a sideways "S" over the white crew neckline. *She never looked better,* he thought. Her fawn-brown hair, swept up in a loose French braid, accentuated the length of her slender white neck, as green and brown tones of shadow gave her hazel eyes a new brilliance. Could he tell her she was a knock-out?

"Are you ignoring me?" she spat. Her auburn lipstick now had the appearance of twisted metal gnawing and lashing.

"Smart mouth…I heard you," he exhaled. "Jackie, get your things. We're leaving. Your mother is having pre-cocktail withdrawal."

The girl giggled and slipped into her room.

"You contribute to this, Zach. I can't believe you allow me…to…to look like a fool in front of our daughter."

"Oh, so now she *is* ours."

"She's yours when she decides to be rude, as you are now."

"Izzy, I'll talk to her. You yourself said she drives you nuts lately. What makes you think you aren't just snapping at things?"

"Fine. Play the weekend father."

Jackie emerged, "See ya," and planted a brief kiss on her mother's cheek before running down the stairs. Isabel continued to sneer at Zach without acknowledging her daughter.

"Have a nice evening, Isabel." Zach put an arm over his daughter's shoulder and escorted her to the door.

"I will," Isabel jeered.

SUBURBAN LIFE STAR: "WHY I ABORTED MY LOVE CHILD"

Gilman filed through Collins' story. It was late. Everyone but the clean-up crew and his secretary were gone. Punching the computer keys, he scrolled the screen up, humming as he went.

He grabbed his coffee mug and took a swig of the lukewarm liquid. "Gad. Marj, get me another cup." He held up the *Pursuit* mug.

His secretary, a middle-aged doting Edith Bunker type, nodded perfunctorily and headed toward the coffee machine.

"Thanks," he muttered, continuing to read the article. He then saved a copy on his hard-drive for the next issue.

Marquel's story was shaping up nicely. It would make a good cover tease alongside Melody's announced pregnancy. A pro and con of sorts.

Collins definitely had following up to do.

Marj handed him a fresh cup. She had been by his side for more than ten years and was efficient, yet demanding of his attention at times. Marj was one step ahead of her boss and leveraged her salary and benefits accordingly.

"The wife went to Syracuse to see her family," Gilman winked. "Want to make it an all-nighter...say, your place in an hour?"

She grinned. She had needs too and he was a steady ride. No hassle, lots of fun and Chinese food delivered. It beat reading or dropping in on the grandkids.

"That's my girl." He cupped a hand over her ass. "I've been dying for some Moo Goo Gai Marj," he squeezed her cheek hard. "God, I've missed you."

CHAPTER FOUR

Isabel's gaze fell over the length of the muscled animal arm in arm with her very best friend. Her eyes trailed the rippling pectorals to the flat of his stomach, on to the bulge just above his thighs. So these were the crown jewels Sophie bragged so much about. She glanced back to meet the man's honey-gold eyes. A mass of raven tousled and moussed hair topped his head. His tanned face, squared and outlined by a clenched jaw, was the poster boy look that made him famous. The pools of liquid topaz were assessing her, taking in the details of her firm, youthful figure.

God, she could drown in those eyes.

She gave him an approving look.

"Sophie, dear…" The women leaned in to touch cheeks. "This must be Sam?" Isabel extended her hand. The man grabbed it briefly and gave her a toothy grin. She should have embraced him, *felt* him.

"Nice place you have here, Isabel." Sam glanced around.

Sophie stroked his hand, nodding to Isabel knowingly.

"Cocktails are out by the pool tonight," Isabel told Sophie. She turned from her guests to the towering silver-haired Lyle. More guests were arriving, and she needed him here for support.

Sophie led Sam out to the bar.

Classes were still in session, Isabel mused. Sophie had schooled so many young men she was nearly an institution unto herself.

Isabel could never understand why young men would bother with Sophie, except for her money. Short and round, Sophie possessed an attractive peach-hue complexion and penetrating robin's egg blue eyes. But her fine platinum hair, bobbed neatly at the shoulder, barely concealed the thick neck that was forever draped in scarves.

She was a sharp wit, never without conversation—always the center of attention. The daughter of a Jewish immigrant and a Georgia belle, Sophie inherited a handsome fortune at the tender age of sixteen. Shortly after her parents died in a train accident, she had moved from Savannah to New York to live with her Jewish grandmother. She later attended Radcliffe, where she and Isabel began a long and sometimes trying friendship.

Isabel was the pretty one, Sophie the smart one. Together they were a mischievous pair, turning things upside down and generally avoiding academic pursuits. Until, of course, they moved on. Life after school was much different. Isabel nabbed Zach. Sophie bought a chain of jewelry stores. Isabel had Jackie. Sophie had her boys. Isabel divorced Zach. Sophie still had her boys. Isabel threw intimate parties. Sophie threw galas.

Things worked out.

Isabel impatiently motioned for Carmen to begin preparing the table for dinner. Ten guests in all. Isabel had invited the crème d'la crème of the current social circuit. Unsophisticated or not, Sam was hot. Hot in the trades and sizzling in full view. How thankful she was that dear Sophie had brought him.

Lyle, of course, would provide the latest studio gossip. Jake Maxwell, a has-been for more the fifteen years and a former 1950's television legend, was back on top again with *Dateline Washington*, a drama series following *Suburban Life* on an opposing network. *Dateline* had already won a loyal following, making the Colbys and Carringtons look like hillbilly cousins. Jake's wife of 35 years was Marilyn Maxwell, Beverly Hills' charity goddess.

While most wives were content to serve with select organizations, Marilyn seemed to take the world on. At near seventy, not looking a day past fifty-five, Marilyn could put a function together in a matter of hours if need be. Rock musicians, actors and media personalities were ever at her disposal. It was even rumored that during Jake's lean years, she took money under the table.

Isabel paced the small foyer. She had managed to nab doctors Mosha and Zena Jain, video fitness gurus, at a Ma Maison luncheon weeks earlier. She was afraid they were a no-show. The two had appeared on nearly every morning show in recent months and just completed transactions on a new clinic on the Avenue of the Stars when Ma Maison owner, Patrick Terrail, introduced them. She owed him for certain, if only they'd get here.

The couple barely took time for video promotions, let alone parties. Isabel's drawing card: none other than Melody Mars. In desperate need of a celebrity spokesperson to advertise their new pregnancy workout, Isabel heartily suggested the expectant cover girl.

Kansas congressman Jim Hanson and his new bride were not only the nation's favorite couple at the moment, but were appearing on a taped Barbara Walters special in a few days.

Isabel had surprised the couple with a gift basket. If only she had that moment on video. Melody got teary-eyed. Jim mumbled. And Sophie threw Isabel their secret *brown-nose* look.

"Ah. Isabel. What type of sausage did you say this was?" Sam chewed loudly as he shoveled the food in his mouth.

"Duck." *You dick. Can't you keep your mouth closed?* Then an evil thought crossed her mind. *Could he be this ravenous in bed?* She turned to Lyle, whose chiseled jaw chewed thirty or forty times before swallowing. His sex was as methodic as his eating habits. *Thrust, thrust, thrust before we bust.*

Boring.

She put her fork down and turned to Melody, who appeared to be a little green at the moment. Would Sophie be hurt if she pursued this sexual monster whose ankles were massaging her own?

Sophie's a big girl. A very big girl, she mused. Her friend didn't have to know.

"Daddy," Jackie propped her chin on the heel of her palm, "can I live with you during the week and visit Mother on the weekends?"

"Baby, why do you ask?" He crossed his arms and leaned against the kitchen counter, glancing occasionally at the hot air popper spewing popcorn into a large aluminum bowl.

"Because. I don't think Mother cares if I'm there or not."

"Visiting her on the weekends would conflict with her social life."

"So! I'd never visit her, then. And why shouldn't she consider your social life?"

"Because you are my social life and she knows it."

"I'm forced to live between two people who have problem schedules."

"Your mother spends lots of time with you."

"Sure. Driving me to the classes she thinks I need. She won't even let me go to the same aerobics class she does. We could do that together. But no, she thinks that would be embarrassing. Unless, of course, one of her friends thought to bring their daughter, then it would be a must."

Zach turned to the bowl and poured melted butter over the fluffed kernels. "Why is this coming up now?" He picked up a few pieces and stuffed them in his mouth, then turned to his daughter and fed her a few.

"Because I don't like it. I'm tired of all this shit. Whose side are you on? You and her have a kid, then, 'til I turn eighteen you get to push me back and forth. It sucks…Oh, and don't forget to speak to me about my smart mouth."

Zach laughed. "I'd rather you express your feelings."

"How about considering them?"

"Okay, what if we make a deal?"

"What kind of deal?"

"If I buy a house in the next year, we'll discuss…with your mother, changing our arrangement. It won't be immediate and just because I decide to look for a house doesn't mean you can pack your bags. Your mother has to be consulted."

"Why a year?"

"Because I don't want you to get anxious. But don't breathe a word to your mother now. She'll think I've concocted the idea to get out of paying child support."

"Really, Daddy. You promise you'll talk to her? And can I go house-hunting with you…please?"

He smiled, handing her the overflowing bowl of popcorn. "I think my best girl could help pick out her new home."

"I like the way you said that. *Home.* What should we watch tonight?" Jackie plopped down on a large portion of the velour pit group. Popcorn fell around her and she began eating the mess. *"Suburban Life?"*

"Fine with me. I hear it's good, but you know me, I'm not up on the tube."

"You're never up on the tube. I have to teach you everything." She lovingly fed her father.

"Well, fill me in on this one…is J.R. going to rob someone of their oil?"

"That was *Dallas.*"

"I give up."

"Okay. This is about a girl, Sharron, played by this cool actress, Marquel. I think that name is so unique. Anyway, Sharron is this funky model who wins contests and is friends with all these screwed up married people. She makes money in bars and clubs and auto shows as a tire model, just showing her bod. There she is…" Jackie pointed to the screen.

"She goes by just *Marquel?*"

"Yeah. Isn't she beautiful?"

Zach stared at the blonde vision on the screen. Jackie definitely had good taste. Of course, half of America had good taste… such brilliant violet eyes. "How long has this show been on?"

"This is the second season. Daddy…don't you ever watch TV?"

"Not so much when you're not around. Just Carson and some old movies. That's about it."

"Old movies. Yuck. You need to enter the real world."

"You need to mind your own business."

"Do you think you'll ever meet Marquel? *Pursuit* had an article about her abortion. Who do you think her doctor is? Sikes?"

"You don't read that trash, do you?"

"Ask Dr. Sikes."

"Patient information is confidential."

"Come on, I won't tell."

"Jackie, I asked you if you read *Pursuit*...does Isabel buy those magazines?"

"They're not magazines, duh! But some of the stuff is true. Like that gay guy, John Spencer, who was hiding his affair with that actor. That was true. He was your patient."

"His homosexuality was no secret. His partner's *was* before that article..."

"Coming out is healthy...you said so."

"When one makes that decision for himself, yes. It's still difficult."

"What about Marquel?"

"I'd like to watch the program. Can we discontinue this discussion?"

"Will you ask Dr. Sikes?"

"No, Jackie. She could be my next-door neighbor for all I know."

"Seriously?"

"Yes."

"Marquel's your neighbor?"

"NO."

"'Cause if you were, I'd go over there. What a trip. My friends would sh..."

"Shit?"

"Sorry, Daddy...and no, Mother doesn't buy *Pursuit*," she lied. Isabel liked reading them, too.

"Who's that guy?"

"Sam Kindred. *People* magazine's 'Sexiest Man Alive', but I'd go for JFK Jr. over him. Hey, why don't you ask the Sellecks over?"

"How did we get onto the Sellecks?"

"Well, Mother is right about one thing…you need to socialize more."

"Watch the show." He placed one hand over the top of her head and turned it toward the television.

Heading north on the Pacific Coast Highway, Ken made a conscious effort not to speak. They would have time for that once they reached The Surf, an inexpensive eatery, where hopefully she wouldn't be noticed. He wanted Marquel to take in the view and unwind—to forget the show. Forget the fucking reporter he'd sent to the studio and just relax.

Christ, how could he have been so stupid? An *abortion* headline! It was that dumb bitch Terry's fault! If she'd ever take a decent message or screen a call properly this wouldn't have happened. He'd get a temp and lay Terry off. Fuck her!

He'd fire her ass. Yeah.

Marquel was his star. His baby. A mother*fucking* star! He couldn't afford to blow this.

He thought about the time she climbed in bed between him and Evan. They'd been cuddling and were becoming aroused when she opened the door. She'd stood there watching them. She complained that she couldn't sleep…

"I'm freezing. I need some warmth. Would you mind if I got in bed with you?"

Evan pulled back the covers and she walked right up the middle of the bed, pushing Ken aside. At first, he considered slapping her. How dare she come between them! She must have been sleepwalking, they both thought, but the next morning was the same. She woke and asked Evan if he'd make her an egg. She was hungry. Ken rolled his eyes and Evan just shrugged.

"Sure, sweetie," Evan kissed her forehead. He stood and stretched. "Daddy will make you French toast if you'd like."

It was then she snapped out of it.

"NO!" She departed from their bed. "I wish everyone would just leave me the hell alone."

"What's gotten into her?" Ken rolled onto his stomach and reached for Evan's thigh.

"She doesn't like French toast?"

"You'd think she was raised in a cave by a pack of wild French toast."

"Like it or not Ken, you've got a problem child." Evan bent over and gave Ken a slap on the ass.

"What could be so bad about French toast? Unless you ran out of syrup! That's it, she grew up so poor that they couldn't afford eggs or syrup, so they *pretended* their toast was French."

"Oui oui."

"Ev, what should…" Evan covered Ken's mouth with his.

Ken swerved to the right, just missing the guard rail.

"Ken?" Marquel grabbed for the dash.

"What?" Couldn't she see he was busy at the moment?

"Ken, you mumbled that Terry was a dumb bitch…"

"Oh my God, I said that out loud?"

"Yes."

Oh, that's right; he was going to fire Terry. Funny thing was it was a dipshit like Terry who called from Florida saying they were sending someone out. God, how lucky he'd been to have a phone number one digit off from Burt Reynolds' agent. The Beverly Hills address had killed his budget, but this coincidence had paid off. Big. The bimbo from Florida sent Marquel right to his door. Thank God.

But it wasn't all roses. Marquel was a nervous wreck. A cruel joke at first, he thought. The big boy giving him shit. But why? He had no one in demand.

Putting her up in Evan's rental was the smartest thing he could have done. A little R&R. A week to adjust and she went out on nearly every call he had word of.

And then it happened.

Suburban Life.

A dream come true.

The bleached blonde from Florida won the role of Sharron. She didn't even have to open her mouth. Ty went nuts. Carnie went nuts. Everyone agreed she was Sharron.

Now earning a hundred G's an episode! He was rolling now. An unknown coming in with no credits and winning the lead. Christ, there was a God. A friggin' *Baywatch* episode and some theater and she was a weekly happening that every casting director wanted. He'd have to ask for twice the amount soon or things could die down.

He steered the Mercedes into The Surf's parking lot.

Not too busy today. He was glad. They needed to talk. Air this *Pursuit* thing out. He didn't want her to think he went for that crap.

Walking up to the restaurant's entrance they didn't say a word. She left her sunglasses on. Seated at a window booth, she pushed her glasses into her hair.

He couldn't figure her out sometimes. She'd talk incessantly some days, and others she just clammed up and stared. Today she didn't even smile, just looked blank. Could he blame her?

"You hungry?" He patted her hand.

"Ken, I don't know why we're here."

"We need to talk."

"Yes, we do. Was Mark Collins your idea of responsible journalism?"

"It was a mistake."

"That's it?"

"Scream. I deserve it. But I had no idea he'd conjure up something this..."

"Conjure? Conjure! You knew he'd make something up?"

"No, of course not. There isn't any truth to it...is there?"

"I'm walking." She rose from the table.

He grabbed her hand. "Honey, I'm tripping over my tongue here. I don't know much about you. I thought maybe something did happen...like some guy getting rid of a good thing...when he didn't know what he had."

She said nothing. A slow smile eased the hard lines of her face.

He felt relief. Most women would have slapped him, but with Marquel he could never tell. Hell, he wondered if *she* knew which way she'd react. That's what bothered him most. There was something out of sorts—not normal—about Marquel. While he wanted to chalk it up to star quality and the eccentricity that went with it, he didn't feel in his gut that her quirks or problems fit the pattern. That was it. It wasn't quirky or problematic; it was something deeper, like an erupting volcano in the early stages.

"I'm sorry." She sat again and glanced out at the ocean.

"No, I'm sorry."

"I've never had an abortion. Never considered such a thing."

"Well, let's not get pregnant." He tapped his nails on the tabletop.

She laughed. "Ken, you amaze me."

He couldn't believe she was laughing. She was calm. Almost happy. He could kiss her.

The waitress handed them each a menu.

"Ken, I don't know…I have days when I don't feel like I *belong*."

"Honey, I feel like I don't. I mean, look who you're talking to. Like before you walked in my door. I wasn't doing any business per se."

"That's not…"

"I have to get rid of Terry and small-timers like her…move forward."

"But I'm not talking about work. I'm talking about California. I feel so alien. I haven't any friends…I don't feel like *we're* friends. I feel you need me, that I'm just a paycheck."

"Of course we're friends," he lied. He felt no more for her than the money she brought him. He wanted to care, but the damn dollar signs always got in the way. What if she did walk? What if she was like all the others? They didn't give a damn what expense he went through to keep them happy.

Did she understand the torture this business brought him? The ass-kissing negotiations?

"I'm sorry, Ken…" She looked out the window. "That magnificent ocean doesn't help…I'd like it to take me away…swallow me up and bury me in its depth…"

God, here we go again. The slap of cold water after the warm bath.

"You know what I mean?" she whispered. She pulled the sunglasses off her head and placed them back over her eyes.

This wasn't good. She was going to cry. He knew. Was she suicidal? Was this one of those warning signs?

"Yeah," he choked. Of course he loved her…in his own way. He didn't want her to suffer. God knew she was mixed up. But why?

He wasn't sure what to do. He had to find her some help. A treatment center or maybe a therapist she could talk to professionally. Someone. Or he was afraid he'd lose her forever.

"Joyce Oswald?"

"Who wants to know? And what are ya doin' calling me so early?"

"Mark Collins with *Pursuit*."

"And?" She could kiss him for that little article he'd written.

"Could we get together? Say, lunch? Discuss matters further…"

"Discuss what? What matters to you or me?"

"Well, I think we could work something out."

"Perhaps we could. What is it ya want?"

"Anything on your co-star."

"Um." She sat up and threw the bedspread off her scantily clad body. He was kind of cute as she recalled…a small but tight ass. She stood and pulled the spaghetti straps of her gown off her shoulders and let the garment fall to the floor.

"I don't care if it's as silly as…eating four Godiva's before each shoot. I want anything I can get." He didn't have to tell her much. She was a talker.

"Why Marquel?"

"Why do people read tabloids? We just give them the people they're interested in."

"So I'm chopped dog shit, eh?"

Yeah. "How about a trade-off...a fashion spread? We've got 'about town' shots in the centerfold."

"Um."

"What's all the 'ums?' You in the middle of something?" Was she screwing someone? Talk about talent. He felt a throb.

"The middle of something?" she laughed. "You interested?"

"Perhaps."

"Perhaps! I don't deal in perhaps. A man's gotta know what he wants."

"Deal me in." He felt himself grow stiff.

"Don't cream your jeans, Collins."

"Screw you."

"You'd like to."

"You'd like me to."

"Enough. I'm not into phone sex."

He smiled.

"Well, I'm glad you have a sense of humor, Collins. We may get along." She stretched, then looked at herself in the mirror. Her heavy breasts sagged a bit; the mere weight pulled them down. Her stomach was flat. She pressed on it and turned sideways to have another look.

She picked up a hand mirror on the bedside table. What awful bags. Too much booze. She needed an ice-cold shower... wake up a bit.

"When should I check back with you?"

"Try a couple of days. We're having a *power lunch* with Carnie tomorrow," she sighed. "He's about ready to throw in the towel. His ulcers will kill him if the show doesn't."

"Where's lunch?"

"Hey, I can't have you tailin' me." She plopped down on the bed and started doing leg raises. "Don't ya trust me?"

He didn't trust anyone. "Okay. I'll call you in a few days."

"Besides, Marquel is schizo over that article. If she sees you and connects us, what do ya think you'll get then? Nothing from me. I'm not stupid…I'm not going to be tagged as your accomplice."

He sighed. "Got the picture. Calm down."

"And another thing, don't you fuckin' tell me to calm down. Who do you think you're talkin' to? You attempt to tell me what to do one more time and I'll chew your balls off with my bare teeth."

"Ouch. Got the picture."

"No, you don't! I said I'd help ya. Anonymously. A source. No quotes. You create trouble for me and your nuts will be hanging from my rearview mirror. You may think I'm some big-titted no-talent, but I'm not lettin' some cub reporter ruin what I've built."

What you've built? He wanted to laugh. What did anyone in this town build, but a list of sex partners who got them to the next level?

He looked at the outline of his fly. She was building him up all right.

"Perfectly understood."

"Fine. Gotta go." She hung up.

Collins closed his eyes, then put the dial tone to rest. *No talent?…Joyce, you have plenty of talent. Talent I can build on,* he groaned.

CHAPTER FIVE

M arquel poured a healthy dollop of sunscreen over her bare breasts. The heat was scorching, suffocating. She must have fallen asleep on the chair. Burning was the only sensation she felt as she lathered the warm liquid over her body.

She was golden. Bronzed. All but a string line up her rear and a small patch in front. Why did this heat give her such a sick feeling? She rubbed the remaining lotion over her hands and tossed the bottle into a canvas bag. She needed to take a stroll, splash off the stinging fire that singed her skin and shake off the impending exhaustion. She grabbed her fuchsia bikini top off the back of the chair. She couldn't bring herself to walk the beach topless. She didn't know why. The area was secluded, all but a sandcastle at the shoreline. Construction had neared completion, she observed. She took a swallow of her mineral water.

She curved her hand over her brow and looked at the mounds again. A few paper cups were tossed aside. The castle molds. The ocean surged just beyond it, keeping a safe distance, chanting its consistent hypnotic howl. She couldn't help but feel drawn in.

Walking over to the sand sculpture, she knelt down. Touching the top of the castle's tower, her fingers lingered there, caressing its grainy surface.

A chill ran through her.

The sun's rays quickly replaced the sensation with welcoming heat.

She sat on her heels, mesmerized by the simple design. Scooping out a moat with the crumpled waxed paper cup, she piled sand onto the tower. It must have been a long time ago, the last time she played like this. She couldn't remember doing such a thing. Or even being a child.

She patted her hand over the sand-filled cup. Many hours had passed, she was certain. Yet time had no place here. The past didn't exist, and the future would never be. The present was the horizon winking its goodnight and the ocean breeze wrapping a chilly arm around her.

Then it seemed to happen out of nowhere. A startling surge washed over the castle's base, filling the moat with a fierce rush. The tide gathered fistfuls of sand and selfishly washed it out to sea.

"No…" Marquel made a sweeping motion, pulling up more sand to fill in the base of the castle.

Digging her knees in, she was determined to pat and reshape the structure before it could be washed away. Yet the ocean fought to recapture its border, pulling with it fragments of sand and shell.

She blinked the salt from her eyes as she felt the wet Pacific bathe her thighs. It was happening too fast.

Tears clouded her vision.

She looked to the cloudless dusk sky, her lips trembling. Throwing herself over the castle, she writhed. The crashing waves mocked her, lathering her with froth, washing over her limp and quivering body as it pulled the earth out from under her.

It was too late.

She couldn't save it.

"Why? Why?" She felt herself heaving, felt the nausea. She had nothing in her system to vomit. She looked up. Naively, she wanted immediate answers. "Am I crazy?" She screamed. "What's the matter with me?"

Hours later she awoke in her car, the sunroof open, her body shaking from the sixty degrees of ocean breeze. She wasn't certain if it was morning or evening. She heard voices and could see two glowing dots off in the distance. A couple walking the beach as they smoked, she guessed.

She shut the roof and went for the ignition, but there was no key in place.

"Shit."

She felt around. Where were they? She rubbed her eyelids with her knuckle and felt the sting of dried salt on her skin. The grains of sand on her hand scratched her face.

"Shit...shit...SHIT!"

She couldn't touch any part of herself. She was human sandpaper. She needed a shower of fresh water and soap, followed by vitamin E and aloe therapy. She got out of the car and stumbled on the sand.

"Christ."

She picked herself up and looked in the back window and saw all her gear piled up. Each item was coated in sand. She opened the door and pulled out the canvas bag. Shaking it off, she dug around for her keys. Relief. She grabbed the key ring and got back in the driver's seat.

It was all okay now. She could go home and things would be okay. *Should* be okay. Okay. *Okay.*

CHAPTER SIX

"When a man loves a woman..." the crooning black singer explained.

Despite Percy Sledge's attempt to reach the very soul, the AM radio continued to crackle and choke his voice.

A cool gust swept through the garage with the imminent smell of rain. A few wrenches squealed in protest while the air compressor hummed a loud, persistent moan.

George looked at the white face clock just beyond the girlie auto parts calendar. Squinting to read the numbers, he was sure the hands would agree with his aching belly that it was time to quit.

6:48 a.m.

Close enough.

He was hungry, damned hungry, and all he wanted to do now was sit in his regular booth and have big, sweet Martha set a plate of eggs and biscuits in front of him. He could taste the biscuits dipped in runny yolks and smell the coffee.

"You done?" A voice called. "Let's grab a booth...they got a new waitress...Tiffany."

The other men mumbled.

A large, burly bald man gestured crudely, "I'd like some Tiffany under me."

Approving laughter.

George ignored them. Walking over to the sink, his white stained t-shirt was loosely fitted into faded Levi's. George was the picture of down home all-American good looks. Scooping a handful of grease cleaner between his palms, he looked in the mirror. *Where did I go wrong?* he wondered. He'd been working in a Gainesville truck depot nearly all his life. Where did it get him? *Thank God for the Gators!* Football was his only vice. A regular at the Chiefland Bar and Grill during football season, George caught only the college games.

His hazel eyes were tired. For a man of thirty-two, they seemed to have weathered twice their years. Seen too much, hurt too much. His straight nose and perfect mouth had also met few smiles these days, other than an obligatory gesture of courtesy to a lady or a forced grin for these bastards.

He didn't give a shit about any Tiffany. He was only interested in his privacy and the daily welcome of large, compassionate, friendly and sweet, black Martha. Things in the South never changed much. Not the roots and rural community. Blacks were separate, but equal. But nevertheless, *separate*. George didn't care much about race, gender or social status. He knew people on both sides of the Rosewood issue and he felt bad that people died. He was a simple man. Intelligent. But not caught up in rumors, television or newspapers. He just wanted to be left alone to hunt, fish and boat along the Waccasassa. The forty-mile commute each way from his Gulf Hammock cabin gave him plenty of time to listen to his Alabama, Hank Williams and Patsy Cline cassettes.

Rinsing the soap between his fingers, he assessed his dried, cracked fists. His nails were caked in grease, and his ring slipped about easily with the lubricant.

He wrung his hands unconsciously, scratching the top of them to get a little soap under his nails. He'd have to sit with these dumb bastards again today or he'd never hear the end of it. Their continuous laughter grated on his nerves.

Ted, in a mock feminine voice called to him. "George, oh George, do wash those big, strong hands for me."

George turned. "You really think that waitress is gonna be turned on by a bunch of grease-coated hard-ons like us?"

Ted threw the small cap that barely covered his hairless scalp to the floor. "I think the wife left you because your pretty boy looks attracted others like yourself."

George swallowed hard. Ted could piss him off easily. He hated how the dumb bastard affected him. "Homo diesel mechanics like you, Ted?"

Ted pirouetted his elephant body around, tiptoed over to George and smeared a greasy hand over his face. "Nice try asshole."

Again, the laughter.

George froze. He could feel his blood pressure rising, but he wouldn't give in to them. Wouldn't give them the satisfaction of displaying more than a streaked, clenched jaw.

"C'mon guys, it's going to be awhile before Georgy gets those zebra stripes off…let's clock out and get us a good seat."

George turned back to the sink and smeared the congealed soap on his face.

Ted and the other walked toward him. The pack seemed determined to see who would get the upper hand, George or Ted.

"Move over pretty boy," Ted sing-songed. Then he leaned in close. George could feel Ted's breath on his neck. "Don't you ever worry that some butt-reaming convict is going to work here someday and get his hands on you?"

"Jesus, Ted! I'm not *Boy* George."

The men seemed to laugh far too long for Ted's patience.

"You mind?" He gestured for George to give him some room at the sink. Ted's wide nostrils flared, his jowl squared indignantly and he squinted at the other men as he looked in the mirror.

CHAPTER SEVEN

M arquel cornered Ken on his way to the bar, grabbing him by the wrist. "Got a minute?"

"For you, doll, anything," he stumbled. "Whoa! A little too much drinkie."

"I've gotta leave a little early." She sipped at her white wine. Her palms were already clammy and cold, her breathing labored. She didn't want to be here.

Ken insisted she make an appearance.

From the outside no one would guess the woman in the green Dior was a wreck. The challis chemise shimmered with each breath she drew, a rippling green river mirroring a luminous full moon.

She was acting her part, though any minute she feared she might hyperventilate and run for the door.

"Have you and Sophie had a confab yet?" He scratched his ass. "God, I think I'm coming down. Let me have that." He grabbed her glass and tossed the liquid down his throat. "I'm a born lush, sweetie...God, I love to drink. Alcohol is the nectar of the God's gods."

He took a red silk handkerchief from the breast pocket of his black Armani suit and mopped his forehead.

Marquel squeezed his wrist. "Don't make an ass out of us."

"Who's representing who here?" he snickered. "Horton hears a who..."

She was infuriated. Shocked at his behavior. She had never seen him so out of control. In fact, she had never seen him out of control at all. She wanted to scream. She could feel her hands starting to tremble.

"Come on, let's get out of here."

A couple passed. They smiled and nodded. She was thankful this corner of the house wasn't heavily traveled.

"I gotta pee," he crossed his legs.

"Go."

"Okay."

He toyed with his fly.

"Ken!"

"*Jee*-sus! I'm just funnin'ya." He pinched her cheek. "Be right back…mingle, mingle."

Marquel held her breath. Ken scurried off like a field rat, peeking in doorways. He darted into one. She hoped it was a bathroom. She also hoped he'd return soon or she would have to leave him.

Thank God she had driven. He had protested, wanting to take a limo instead.

He'd probably never miss her. She'd give him ten minutes, tops. She noticed Sophie and Jake, arm in arm, approaching.

"Marquel, dear, have you and Jake had the pleasure?"

Fortunately, *no*.

She smiled, extending her hand to the aging actor, which he took rather ceremoniously, kissing her palm as though she should be grateful.

"A rival."

She nodded.

"Too bad soaps aren't like the NFL; we could trade our Tim Barton for your Sam Kindred…"

"Sorry about the Golden Globe." She referred to Jake's losing to Sam.

He ignored her, turning to Sophie. "Where's that columnist?"

"We'll grab him in a bit." She winked at Marquel. "First, we three should become better acquainted."

Here it comes, Marquel thought. The Dior seemed to tighten and constrict, as though she were being swallowed by a large green snake.

She'd like to tell Jake Has-Been where he could go and Sophie not to bother including her in the conversation.

Jake took a long pull of his scotch and looked around, as if surveying the nouveau-Kyoto interior.

Sophie leaned in close, whispering to Marquel. "He's scared shitless the sweeps will bury his ass and leave yours afloat."

Marquel smiled weakly. Lifting her empty glass to Jake, she made a silent toast to finding the nearest exit.

Jake turned back and his gray eyes gave her a once over. He waved to someone in the distance. Taking Sophie's arm, he began to lead her away, giving Marquel a knowing nod.

Sophie grinned and put a hand on Marquel's shoulder. "We'll chat soon."

Relief. Marquel exhaled, then gulped in another breath.

It was odd. Sophie seemed genuinely nice…if that was possible.

Ken returned from the restroom looking weird. He burst out laughing wildly. "Calgon, take me away!"

"Out!" She pointed to a nearby hallway.

"Mark," Sophie touched cheeks with the reporter. "How sweet of you to come."

"*Pursuit* wouldn't dream of disappointing you." Mark Collins held onto her right hand.

"You could never disappoint me. However, my guests are another story." She dug her talons into his palm. "You've ruffled more than a few feathers lately."

"Are you suggesting I watch my step?" He gave her a clenched-teeth grin. In spite of the pain, he managed a poised smile.

"On the contrary. I'm merely stating fact. It's entirely up to you whether you value your welcome in this town."

He laughed. "My welcome?" She had to be kidding. Welcome…what good was it? Who needed a friggin' welcome to do a story?

"You're amused?"

"Extremely."

"Tell me, Mark, don't you ever get just a little concerned about *Pursuit's* content? Your work does seem to border on the dark side."

"Can't make money writing good news," he shrugged.

"You've quite a sense of humor."

"I've been considering stand-up."

"Ah, so this is part of your…routine."

"No routine, Sophie. I just observe."

"How is it you observe things in such a distorted fashion?" She let go of his hand abruptly.

"Distortion is in the eye of the beholder."

She swung her head back in laughter. "Yes. I see what you mean."

Collins motioned for his photographer. "Dave."

The short, long-haired man stomped over. "Yo."

"A few shots of Ms. Krentz and Jake together."

Dave nodded to the two. He was a man of few words.

"Mark," Sophie interrupted. "Make sure you get a good photo of Marquel. She's around somewhere."

He turned instinctively, as if expecting to find the actress standing behind him.

"It'll be our pleasure." He dug his hands in his pockets and walked toward the next room.

Jake slapped Sophie on the ass. "Soph, the paparazzi is waiting."

"Ouch." She spun on her heel.

"Think we can manage a candid pose?" Jake belted out a laugh.

"Do your usual wooden Indian, I'll pretend to look interested."

"The kidder!" He slapped the small of her back, catching her off guard.

Sophie hadn't time to think. Her mouth flew open in an "OH!" as the camera shutter released.

Jake wailed in laughter.

"No bullshit shots…I'll fucking ban you from this place!" She lunged for Dave.

Another flash blinded her.

Jake was wheezing. "What…a sense of humor?"

"*You're dead!*" Sophie screamed at the photographer.

Jake's eyes streamed tears, his tan face turning redder.

"And you," she turned to Jake. "I'd kick you right in your rotten, dried-up balls if it weren't for the fact that I respect your wife."

Dave retreated hastily, slugging camera equipment as he ran.

"Stop him!" Sophie screamed, her apricot complexion turning the scarlet of her paisley print scarf.

Two of the boys went after Dave, knocking Collins against the wall.

"What the...?"

Sophie stumbled after them, losing a shoe along the way.

"What's the problem?" Collins asked Sophie.

"He took one of those damned gag shots...I'll have your ass if it runs!"

He stifled a laugh. "It won't"

"Get me that film or get the hell out."

Within minutes two brawny bodyguards carried Dave back.

"Dave, what the hell's gotten into you? Give her the film," Collins said, pretending to scold his friend.

"What the fuck for?" Dave asked as he dangled it mid-air. The thugs refused to put him down.

"The lady asked for the film." He nodded toward Sophie.

"*And?*" the short man spat.

"And if you don't, King Kong and Mighty Joe Young will toss our asses out."

"Fine."

"Fuckin' hand me the film, Dave."

"Freedom of the press."

"Give the lady her film."

A small crowd gathered around them. A few of Dave's compadres were snapping his photo.

"Okay." It seemed to come from nowhere.

"Thanks." Collins sighed too quickly in relief.

"Let's return the precious film," Dave unloaded the camera, "to the *nobody*."

"That's it!" Sophie shrieked. "Get them out. But get the film first! It's been nice, Mark." She turned and exited down the narrow hall.

"Great fuckin' deal Dave."

Herb Green, a tall, lanky redhead with the freckled looks of an aging Howdy Doody, approached the tee. Jim Sikes, Lou Bartalow and Zach Manning stood off to the side watching their fellow physician's precision swing.

Their eyes followed the orbiting golf ball.

"Sikes, never in your dreams." Herb jumped up. "Try and top it."

Jim ran a hand over his chin. "I'm surprised those bony arms don't fly off and follow that ball."

"Jealous bastard," Herb grinned. His freckled, red-mopped head nodded. "So, how is the pussy factory these days?" He grabbed Jim's shoulder. "We haven't had a report. Come to think of it…you should be wearing your rubbers out here ol' boy. It couldn't hurt your game."

"Speaking of probing," Lou waved his hands, "how about a game show where blindfolded GYNs put on their gloves to battle for cash and prizes on…don-*da*!…Name That Vagina! Sorry Dr. Sikes, but that was Mrs. Harvey Wallbanger for 50."

Zach pushed a thumb and forefinger under his sunglasses, pinching the bridge of his nose as he laughed. "Sikes…"

Jim approached the tee. Lou, Herb and Zach tried to hold in their laughter. Jim turned. "I'm trying to concentrate."

They all backed up. "All yours pal," Herb said. The three looked at each other and busted out laughing. Sikes was the worst golfer they knew. Helluva doctor, but a lousy golfer.

"Christ. Why do I bother?" Jim was pissed.

"Because, Sikes, we're jealous as hell. You fondle women all day and get paid for it! All we do is analyze them, drill their teeth and remove their spleens. You know damn well women love their GYNs more than their husbands. Now hit the fucking ball!"

CHAPTER EIGHT

A trill convulsed Ken out of a deep sleep.
"Oh, God." He sat up.

His heart beat wildly against his ribcage. His hands trembled as he tried to remove the black satin sleep mask. The digital clock read 3:23 a.m. He grabbed the receiver. "Hello?"

A weak voice sobbed across the line. He immediately thought of Terry, with her breathless, hushed tone.

"I can't hear you...speak louder."

"Kelly's...wants to..."

"Kelly who? Wants to what? Who is this?" Ken ran his fingers through his hair. "You must have the wrong number."

"Ken?"

It was Marquel. She sounded drugged, out of it.

"Marquel, are you okay?" God, what's wrong with her? "Do you want to come over? Are you in trouble?" She's losing it. He sank back into the mountain of pillows. She's really losing it. Probably about to overdose.

She whispered something unintelligible.

"Speak louder...what is it? What?"

"I'm okay, I...I had a bad dream. That's all." She started to cry again. "I can't remember anything about...the dream. I just have this sick feeling."

"I'll call a doctor." He too had a sick feeling.

"No. Please, I'll be all right." She yawned.

71

"Marquel, you mentioned someone…a Kelly, when I answered."

"Kelly who?"

He rolled his eyes. *I'm* the one having a nightmare. "Honey, forget it. I'm coming over." He was sure she had taken something. She must have, why else all the weird talk?

"No."

Was this her idea of a last farewell? "No can do, doll. I'm coming…we'll have breakfast, a regular pajama party."

"I must have dialed in my sleep, Ken. I'm fine…really it was only a dream. Let's both get some rest." She yawned again

How can I friggin' sleep now? "I'm not letting you go until you answer a question for me. Honestly. Did you take anything? Sleeping pills, valium, anything?"

Another yawn. "NO…I'm…I had a nightmare, okay?"

"You sure?"

"Of what?"

"That I shouldn't come over?"

"Very."

Jesus, how could he let her hang up? "Call me if you need me. Promise?"

"Promise."

"I care…"

"Goodnight." She hung up.

Ken reached for Evan's arm. His lover slept soundly. He thought about putting on a pot of coffee and talking, but instead he put his sleep mask back on and curled up next to Evan. He knew what he had to do. There was no question. This call confirmed his deepest concerns. She could be suicidal.

CHAPTER NINE

"Terry," Ken spoke into the intercom, "hold all calls."

Angel voice. "Yes, Mr. Avery."

He had fired her a week earlier, hiring a highly recommended executive secretary, who, it turned out, only wanted one thing… his Rolodex.

After "Highly Recommended" made off the with master, and literally every important connection he had, he felt forced to get Terry back.

Granted, she was stupid, but trustworthy. At a time like this, trust was all that mattered. But worse still, he had to go to a Safeway store where she was cashiering and beg her to come back.

"I like it here." She pushed the food across the electronic scanner. Her wisps of honey-blonde hair were pulled back into a ponytail, making her full mouth and almond-shaped eyes resemble those of a freshly-painted porcelain doll.

He squinted, pursing his lips. "Terr…this is show biz we're talking about. You don't wanna be bagging Dorito's and fish sticks the rest of your life."

"You called me a bimbo."

"I'm sorry. I was frustrated. How about a raise?"

"I make good money here. And I get benefits, y'know. Insurance, stuff like that."

"Okay, insurance. You got it."

"Could I go to some parties too?"

"I'll consider it," he lied. He couldn't have Baby-Jane Mansfield running her mouth to just anyone.

"That'll be $51.92."

"Christ." He handed her a fifty and a twenty. "Can you actually make change?"

"See, you're insulting me again."

"No, Terry. I always buy my office supplies at a Carmel Safeway. Do you know how far my office is from here? Look who I'm asking...what's your answer? You with me or not?"

"With." She rolled her eyes. "I don't like standing, anyway."

"Good. Clock out, we're leaving."

"But..."

"Stand or sit, baby. You decide."

"It's not right."

A low grumbling voice came from behind him. "You're damn straight it ain't right. She's ringing me out first." The pro wrestler figure eyed Ken.

Ken waited in the car an hour before Terry emerged. No matter, it was a relief to have her back.

He held the phone away from his face and mocked the recorded music. The call service picked up. "...Dr. Manning is with a patient. May I take a message?"

Ken put the phone to his ear. "Ken Avery. See if he'll take my call. Lou Bartalow referred me."

"One moment."

Ken sharpened a pencil in the electric sharpener on his desk. "Zach Manning."

"Zach, this is Ken Avery of Preferred Talent. I need to schedule an appointment for a client of mine...She doesn't know I'm contacting you...I won't waste your time...I think she may be suicidal..."

"Perhaps you should take her to a psychiatric hospital and see if she'll voluntarily admit herself."

"It isn't going to be *that* easy, Zach. I'm assuming you know crazy people better than I do."

"Crazy people?"

"You know what I mean. How does one know if what they suspect to be a sign of depression is actually depression or eccentricity?"

"Why do you think your client is suicidal?"

"She's not happy. Well, who is? But, she's off in another world. I know it isn't drugs."

"How can you be certain?"

"I *do* drugs, Zach. She's seen me with drugs and she's not interested. In fact, she lectures me about my drug use."

"She may be depressed. That doesn't mean she wants to kill herself."

"Well, you are the expert."

"Let's make this simple. Lou referred you, so I'll connect you to my secretary and she'll schedule your client. What is her name?"

"Is your secretary to be trusted? This has got to remain confidential."

"Of course."

"For your records, please make her Betty Smith, but it's Marquel, of *Suburban Life*. You're familiar with the series?"

"Yes." A surprised smile grew on Zach Manning's face.

"You can understand my dilemma."

"And she doesn't know you're contacting a psychiatrist?"

"I'm sure she'll see you. She does trust me."

"I'm glad to hear that."

Dr. Manning had a smooth, reassuring sound. Ken wondered for a moment if the doc would like a voiceover career.

"I'm going to connect you with my secretary. It'll be a couple of weeks. I'm booked solid. Unless you want to take her to the hospital?"

"Weeks? Lou said you'd help me out…work her in. Didn't I say suicide, pal? What would it look like if you had her death on your hands?"

"Threatening me?"

75

"No, but I'm desperate."

"There are hospitals that can admit her immediately, but I'll see what I can do. Mr. Bartalow doesn't know my schedule. Did you reveal your client's name to Mr. Bartalow?"

Ken felt a flush in his face. "Yes."

"So much for confidentiality."

"He's a talker?"

"No Ken, he's not. But how many people are *you* going to talk to?"

"You're pissing me off." Ken broke his pencil in half.

"You aren't the patient, Ken. How can I help her if everyone knows before she does, that this appointment has been set? Talk to her, Ken. Then if she wants to call me, I'll take it from there."

Ken fished the remote out of his desk. Turning the television on, he flipped through the channels, stopping at a cartoon.

"Ken? I'm busy. What is that noise?"

"I'm thinking." He also realized the Roadrunner was now making a "beep, beep" in the background.

"You're wasting my time."

Ken tapped his nails on the intercom. "Zach," he punched off the television, "can you work her in this week? You'll understand when you see her."

"Friday at one." He had an appointment with a Realtor, but it could wait. "Are you sure she'll make it?"

"To the appointment?"

"Yes."

"I feel confident she will."

"Cheer up Ken; it has to be Marquel who wants to get her life in order. You're trying to help the best that you can."

Easy for you to say, *your* income depends on her staying nuts. "I need her well, Zach. I'm sure you understand."

"Yes."

"Are you available for lunch today, because I'd really like to explain some things. It might be helpful. How about the Polo Lounge in an hour?"

"This isn't necessary," Zach sighed audibly. "You haven't even talked with Marquel."

"You have to eat, Zach. Besides you could advise me about the best way to broach the subject."

"Fine, I'll see you in an hour. I have a two-thirty."

"Great."

Zach hung up. He was actually excited about meeting the actress. Maybe she'd be someone he could really help. For a change.

"Joyce...how do...ooh, that's great...you expect me to...talk?" Collins groaned.

"Kid...if I can...talk...through a...blow-job...so can you."

He lurched, his body quivering in ecstasy.

"Well, it ain't over yet." Joyce slapped him on the ass. "You got yours, but I want mine. I don't know why some women stop when the guy is satisfied."

"Mutual gratification?"

"No such thing. Someone is always the first to climax and then the other one is left to ask for more." She pushed him off of her and proceeded to straddle his chest.

"Give me a minute, will you?"

"Collins, you surprise me. I didn't think you would be up to this much. Sweetheart, you've got stamina. I like that in a man."

He closed his eyes. The sheets were soaked, and the room swam in the musky scent of perspiration and lovemaking. "I think it's about to drop off. I don't know about stamina...but I'd die a happy man."

She rocked her hips forward. "I'm looking forward to a little happiness myself."

The Galleria was wall-to-wall people on Saturday afternoon. Shoppers sauntered by casually, looking in shops, while others bustled by hurriedly.

Marquel pushed the black fedora down to conceal her blonde locks. Walking close to the store entrances, she remained edgy. She kept her head down, focusing on the toes of her black boots that were otherwise hidden by a full-length tapestry skirt. She pushed the dark wayfarers up on her nose. The aroma of coffee drew her into a nearby specialty store.

A childlike shyness possessed her. The effort to order seemed enormous. She glanced around at the displays, decorative mugs and tea cozies. She slowly made her way toward the counter, fishing some change out from her skirt pocket. She stared intently at the blackboard menu.

"Can I help you?" The clerk asked.

"I'd..." She didn't have time to finish before a man stepped around her.

"Yeah, I need an espresso to go." He turned and winked at her.

She stepped back a few paces, realizing the clerk had addressed the man, not her.

"Oh gosh," the man said, "did I cut in front of you?"

She shook her head. He couldn't see the tears behind the dark lenses. The embarrassment squeezed her heart.

"What can I get you?" The next clerk asked.

"Just a regular coffee," she whispered.

She paid and took the cup to a stand that contained sweeteners and creamers. She wanted to stay, just sit at a table and relax, but it didn't feel right. She had to leave the mall before she felt more anxiety or someone discovered her.

Her feet were heavy. She wondered when she last ate. She couldn't remember. Her temples hammered in and out, her vision fading and refocusing with each throb. She tried to breathe through her nose to keep from hyperventilating, but it wasn't working.

She paused; her eyes narrowed on a kiosk of college football jerseys. She took a slow, deliberate sip. Her nose began to run. The tears welled up again.

She turned abruptly, catching her reflection in a shop window. The grim line of her mouth, the contrast of the black hat and glasses against her pale skin and hair made her stop and stare. She almost didn't recognize herself. In fact, she didn't.

CHAPTER TEN

George slid into his regular booth by the window. He glanced out, watching trucks pull in, nodding to a few drivers who recognized him.

"Hiyah, Georgie." The bouncy waitress beamed at him. "I traded with Martha. She don't mind, y'know?"

"I'm flattered, Tiffany…I'm also tired. Bring me my usual."

She pushed the fine blonde strands away from her eyes. "I thought you might like somethin' different today."

"No." Martha would have already brought him his coffee.

"I see ya got a ring on…the good ones are always taken."

He tried to smile. He failed.

"But Tif doesn't discourage easy, know what I mean?"

He knew.

"Hey Tif!" Ted called from the entrance.

She squealed. "Hi fellas!" She waved. "I'm tryin' to get familiar with Georgie."

George folded his arms in anger. His worn denim jacket was the tough skin that kept him insulated from the outside elements.

"Stop messin' with the man. Now, move." Martha interrupted, pouring him some coffee.

"Hey, we traded." Tiffany pouted.

"Honey, leave this man alone, hear?"

"Hear?" Tiffany mimicked, sashaying back to her station.

"Thanks Martha." George felt like kissing the woman. "Don't ever leave me with that blonde uzi again."

Martha laughed. "That girl thinks you're fine. I can't hold her down."

"Well, she noticed my ring."

The gentle woman sighed, lines formed on her sympathetic forehead. "Someone's gonna tell her 'ventually."

George rubbed his tired eyes. Great, then she'll never leave me alone.

CHAPTER ELEVEN

Zach escorted his daughter into the country club ballroom. He couldn't help noticing how gorgeous she was all decked out in a ballerina cut, melon chiffon. He was glad she had talked him into taking her, and he told her so in a whisper.

"Me too, Daddy."

He surveyed the room. "You're the most beautiful girl here." The fact seemed obvious to him.

She blushed. "Thank you. You're the most handsome father."

He grinned sheepishly. "I'm sorry I chickened out of last year's father-daughter dance."

"It's okay."

"Thanks baby." Without thinking, he reached over to muss her hair. The look on her face stopped him cold.

"My hair, Daddy."

Zach shoved his hands in his tuxedo trouser pockets. "Sorry."

She sighed in relief. "No problem, just not the hair, not tonight. Oh God, there's Marnie! Be back in a minute." She ran toward the girl dressed beyond her years in a flaming red strapless gown.

Zach watched the girls greet one another before making his way to the bar.

"What'll it be, Dr. Manning?"

"Scotch, with ice."

"Coming up."

He sipped at the drink as he strolled over to a table of hors d'oeuvres.

"Zach, my man." Herb Green slapped him on the back.

He turned around to face the red-haired man. "What're you doing here? Your kid's only nine."

"Yeah, and her mother knows how to twist an arm. Listen, you free on Thursday? I've got a friend who can set us up in an oil deal, cheap. Interested?"

"No, I'm afraid not."

"Why? It's just a minimum ten to get in and we don't have to put it up for another month."

"I'm in over my head now. Besides, I'm going to sell the condo...or lease it."

"Sell. C'mon, Zach. Get in on this deal before it passes you by."

"Daddy!" A small voice shouted.

"Hello, Amy," Zach addressed Herb's diminutive daughter, a small, feminine replica of himself; red hair and freckles encased in a long, lanky frame.

"Hello, Dr. Manning."

"You look lovely tonight." Her board-thin body was wrapped in baby blue taffeta.

Amy blushed. "Where's Jackie?"

"She's with Marnie, over there."

"I'm going to check it out." She shook her curls in an affirmative nod.

"Don't be long, Amy, and behave yourself."

She squinted at her father, her hands on her hips, then turned and stormed off.

"So, Zach...are you with me?"

"I just declined. Are you hard of hearing?"

"What if I put in your ten and you pay me back?"

"Put in twenty for yourself and leave me out."

"Zach," Herb started whining, "I hate to leave a buddy out. Remember when Isuzu first came on the market? I twisted your arm and it paid off. Big."

"Herb, Isuzu was the only hunch that paid."

"Thanks a whole hell of a lot."

"I didn't come here to talk business. I came to be with my daughter. You should do the same."

"What? Are we bucking for Father of the Year?"

Zach laughed, then sipped his scotch. "Try Father of the Day."

"See ya, Zach." Green turned away.

Zach couldn't help but laugh to himself. The father-daughter redheads were more alike than they realized. He glanced at Jackie and Marnie, who appeared to be generally ignoring Amy. Zach decided he'd better check on the girls.

"Daddy, Marnie said her parents are sending her to Paris for modeling classes this summer. Can I go too?"

He laughed quietly. "Absolutely not. Do you honestly expect me to trust the entire population of French men with my only daughter?"

"Daddy! Really…"

"It's all chaperoned, Dr. Manning," Marnie chimed in.

"I've heard that song and dance before. No way."

"Then you take us, Daddy."

"If I took you to Paris, it wouldn't be for modeling. It would be for cultural purposes. Besides, trips like that have to be planned."

"I wish I could go," Amy chirped.

Jackie took her father by the arm, leading him to a fairly isolated corner. "Daddy, I am so embarrassed. Marnie's parents think she's mature enough to go, and you're treating me like I'm Amy's age."

"Baby, I'm not Marnie's parent and I'm not trying to compete with her parents. Someday you'll understand my reasoning."

Jackie pursed her lips. She looked so much like her mother at that moment that Zach had to remind himself she was not an adult.

"I love you, Daddy…"

"I love you too."

"Please, I wasn't finished."

"I'm sorry. Go on."

"Okay, maybe I can't go to Paris, and maybe I'll live through this, though I don't believe I'll ever understand it. But, couldn't you, maybe, pull some strings?"

"You're not still talking Paris?"

"Forget it," she sighed. Then teasingly, "I'd rather you figure out a way to introduce me to Marquel."

"Mar...? Honey, I..."

Jackie grabbed at his lapels. "You've met her, haven't you?"

She knew him too well. His face said it all.

"No."

"I can't believe this!" She squealed delightedly. "You've met Marquel! She's your patient."

"Shhh." Zach took her by the shoulders. "There's such a thing as doctor-patient confidentiality."

"Oh, is she really sick? God, I hope she doesn't lose..."

"I cannot and will not discuss this with you."

"Oh, this is great, I can't believe it. Wait til I tell..."

"*No one.* You can't tell anyone about this."

She looked down at her feet, sulking. "Damnit. I know I can't tell anyone, but...just *damnit!*"

"Don't talk like that."

"I'm sorry." She smiled. "I hope I get to meet her someday."

He hadn't seen Jackie light up like this in months. He watched her return impulsively to her friends, suspecting she wouldn't be bringing Paris up for quite a while.

Christ, these people are simple, Collins thought. He'd been traveling by car since he arrived in Florida a few days earlier, and he'd yet to secure a single lead from any of these crackers.

The information he'd gotten from the Burt Reynolds Theater was information he already knew: a clip from the production of *My Fair Lady* and a bio that said nothing—this had been her debut. It listed her hobbies and little else.

He had managed to track down a local cast member who had taken her in during the production, but all the ditz came up with was that she thought she heard Marquel say she was form Ocala.

So here he was, on a stretch of highway surrounded by orange groves, on his way to Ocala. He pulled over at a pay phone to call Gilman.

"I've reached a dead-end."

"How?!"

"Can't seem to get more than we've already got."

"Bullshit! Who have you talked to?"

"Theater P.R. and a former roommate."

"Pay the roommate to talk. Tell her we want to take photos of the place they shared and tell her it'll be worth her while."

"She's got nothing to say, Gilman."

"She will for the right amount."

Collins held the phone away from his ear; the old man was really pissing him off.

"I'll talk to you in a few days, give you what I got."

"It better be good!"

Collins slammed the receiver into the cradle. Great, back to Jupiter.

CHAPTER TWELVE

The waiting room was unusually cold, as if the air had been intentionally turned down to 60 degrees. Then again, maybe the chill came from within. Marquel shivered, hugging her arms and rubbing them.

She'd worn old, patched jeans and the Rams football jersey Ken had loaned her the first night she'd come to town. It had served as a sleep shirt ever since, but she'd chosen it today as a disguise, since the large shirt hung loosely over her body. Unfortunately, the clothes she wore seemed to accentuate the mystery of her vulnerable curves even more.

"Smith," she told Zach's secretary, while she shifted her weight to her toes and back to her heels again. A brass and oak plate announced the middle-aged brunette's name as Annet Bailey.

"If you'll just fill out these forms, as much as applies." Ms. Bailey acknowledged her discreetly, passing her a cold, white clipboard and a pen.

Marquel pushed the oversized sunglasses into her hair and glanced at the forms. "Is this necessary? I may only be making the one visit."

"A brief history helps us to serve your needs better. Just for our records. As I said, you need only add what you feel applies."

We? Our? Who was this lady, Manning's mistress?

Marquel sighed and walked over to a group of swivel chairs. What did it matter? All this game playing was pure nonsense. She didn't even know if she wanted to see this doctor. He was probably a grumpy, gray-haired, know-it-all. She glanced at the wall clock, 12:45. He was probably still at lunch. If only Ken would stop trying to live her life…No, that was wrong…he was trying to help her. She had to admit, she needed help. Ken wasn't the only one who had noticed her inability to cope. She could only hope this session would do the trick.

She finished the form, thinking only for a second about throwing the clipboard down and running out.

She returned the clipboard and its forms to the secretary-mistress.

"Dr. Manning will be with you in just a moment." Warm smile.

"Thank you." *This lady was a professional,* Marquel thought. Surely she could turn that smile on and off like a spigot. As she turned her back and walked slowly toward the swivel chairs again, she could swear she felt Ms. Bailey's eyes on her, believing she was crazy.

Instead of sitting, she picked up a magazine and pretended to thumb through it. She turned slightly, so she could see the secretary and the mysterious door to her left. The door opened. Her heart pounded suddenly. She didn't want to look. She wanted to run like hell.

The man approached. "Ms. Smith?"

She turned toward him, eyes downcast. Pulling the sunglasses off, she tilted her head to look at him. His eyes were black, warm and sincere.

He was caught off-guard at the sight of her…here, in this office. Such beauty. Her eyes, the color of lush California grapes, held as much mystery. He hadn't expected this, for everything to be so evident in her gaze. It was almost as if she was crying out for reason, yet she hadn't made a sound.

The curve of her upper lip gave her a precocious, little girl quality. Her nose was straight, delicately bulbed, and Jesus, he was starstruck.

"I'm Dr. Zachary Manning." He extended his hand.

She looked at it uncertainly.

"Where are my manners? Please, let's go into my office."

CHAPTER THIRTEEN

The conversation began slowly. Marquel was polite but guarded.

Zach took a casual approach, skirting the issue instead of attacking it head-on.

He was mesmerized by her. He stared openly as she paced back and forth, running her hands through the curtain of platinum waves. Occasionally she would grab at her oversized shirt, wringing it unconsciously, like a fidgeting child.

She turned to him. Tears spilled from eyes that had become the color of black grapes.

"You see, Doctor, I don't know where to begin." She lit a cigarette and inhaled deeply.

He watched as she lowered herself onto the sofa. He felt for her; her hands trembled so. "Have you ever sought counseling before?"

Her laugh was nervous. She chewed at a hangnail. "I...I don't know. I seem to have a problem with my memory."

He nodded. "All right. Blocking memories isn't uncommon." Where was he going with this? His nerves felt raw from excitement. His behavior was stupid.

"I need help." Her voice cracked. "There are so many things I just don't understand. I did a show in Florida, then I came out here to...to be a star, I guess. Everything else is a blank. I don't know if I had a mother, a brother...friends."

"Do you want to remember these things, or are you afraid of the knowledge it might bring?" He leaned toward her. "I'm certain you'll begin to remember things at some point. Then the floodgates will open…"

"How can you be sure? What if I have amnesia?"

"It's not impossible, but it's also not likely. If you had amnesia it is likely that you would have suffered some kind of brain injury. You would've been in a hospital…there would be records. Do you remember a hospital?"

She shook her head, thinking over what he had said. "No, I remember my first audition. That's it."

"Amnesia isn't likely. It's a little overused in films and novels. I believe psychological trauma, which is also considered a cause for amnesia…"

She laughed bitterly. "Isn't that what I'm experiencing now?"

"Is it?"

Hands shaking more now, she crushed out the cigarette in the marble ashtray. "I…I'm scared." She stood up and walked to the window, keeping her back to him while she spoke. "I feel as though I came here for a reason…Can I go back to where I came from…wherever that may be?" Her voice was breaking and she didn't want to cry again. Ever. "But what you said, trauma, you know? What if something terrible happened in my past? Then I don't think I could go back. I mean, could I? And that would mean that I don't belong here either."

For a moment he wondered if he could treat her effectively. "Marquel…"

She turned to him abruptly, as if hearing her name was a shock. He wasn't sure what he was going to say. Maybe he should refer her to someone else…

"I had this dream, and I called Ken, my agent." She reached up and hooked her thumbs through the worn belt loops of her jeans. Her eyes were glassy and unreadable. "He said I was talking about a Kelly, but I don't know a Kelly. Then something hit me the other day, it was like a flashback, if there is such a thing… I…I believe my mother must have called me Mar-kelly or Kelly."

"Marquel isn't a stage name?"

"I was sure it was, and now this memory..."

"What about your last name?"

"Chapman. I think it's a stage name. I used it in Florida. I dropped it when I came here."

He rubbed his hand over his chin. There was still a feeling of sinking, as if he were in over his head. Perhaps unlocking the door to the unknown, in this case, would be beyond his capabilities. If he unleashed the past and she couldn't work, then the studio and Ken would be looking for recompense. The name alone wasn't much to go on...but it was something, at the very least. "Please, sit for a moment."

She sank into the leather couch, looking up at him.

"Let's work on one thing at a time. You arrived in California as Marquel Chapman?"

"Yes. I have a driver's license and a car registered in that name."

"Do you know your date of birth?"

"Seven, five."

"You're positive of this?" No actress wanted to give the year.

"How positive can I be, Dr. Manning? I remember the numbers, I remember my name. I can't explain why, but they're very clear to me. Sometimes I..." she broke off as if she were uncertain what she was going to say.

"Go on."

"Sometimes I can hear my mother's voice, like I'm remembering something she might've said to me. A response. But it could...I might just be making it up. Like a fantasy, like I'm grasping at straws."

"What do you see when you...when you're hearing her voice?"

"Shadows. A spring afternoon, and she's just a shadow, talking to me quietly, soothingly."

"Close your eyes."

She obeyed.

"What does she look like?"

"I can't see her clearly; the sun is too bright."

"Is she talking to you? What is she saying?"

"She's…she's singing to me. Mar-kelly-welly…of my belly." She smiled. Her eyes flew open suddenly, startled at the realization. She put the back of her hand to her mouth to stifle a sob, her eyes brimmed with tears. "I can *hear* her saying that."

Zach, too, was surprised. He was torn as to whether she should be pressed to probe deeper. He wanted to be certain she was remembering…not conjuring up fantasies.

He cleared his throat. "What else do you recall?"

She shook her head stoically.

"Please, sit back. Relax."

Leaning back as he suggested, she closed her eyes. She tried desperately to regain the image; she yawned. Everything was making her nervous. She could see…a vision…a handsome man in faded denim. He disappeared before she could make out the face…he could've been someone she saw at the supermarket, anyone.

"Nothing's coming to me."

"Are you sure?"

"I thought I saw…a man. But it was nothing, really. I might've passed him in the hall on the way here."

"Wouldn't you remember that?"

"How would I know?" She was puzzled by the question. "I mean, how can I be sure of anything I…" Suddenly she felt angry. The deep purple of her eyes bore into him. "Would I be here if I were sure of myself?"

She stood and reached over the coffee table, grasping a stainless-steel lighter, then retrieved a cigarette from a slender package inside her purse. She didn't bother to look at Dr. Zachary Manning. It was obvious she was angry. Angry at him, angry at herself.

"I know this is difficult for you."

She inhaled a long drag and looked at him. "*Difficult?* Difficult…" She began laughing hysterically. "I don't fucking know who I am…Difficult? Nah. Come on, Dr. Manning, laugh with me."

The redness in her eyes revealed her anguish, her pain. It was more than he could bear.

She coughed.

"Would you like to stop now? Maybe reschedule?"

"Perhaps I should just leave," *and never come back.* "But before I do, tell me something…what do you see here? What am I?" She was calm now. "Give me something to go on."

He put his hands together in his lap. "I see a woman who needs therapy, possibly hypnotherapy. You want so badly to remember…it may be you're stifling a memory that you don't want to live up to. It may not be as bad as you fear it is, but people who block out a portion of their life usually do so to escape something. I think you'd agree we need to find out what that is."

She listened, not buying it all. She was hurt and angry. "What's next?"

"You have some more time today. What do you think? Discuss things further? Maybe take a different approach?"

"For instance?"

"Let's discuss what you would call an ideal childhood."

"Why?" She inhaled again, then crushed out the cigarette.

"It might help your memory, setting the stage for what you wish had been your childhood."

"I don't really understand this…" She settled back onto the couch, pulling her legs up underneath her, Indian style. "How far back?"

"As far as you'd like."

"The womb?"

"If you wish."

"Okay, the womb." She laughed nervously. "I've always thought of the womb as a washer or dryer…where you might lift up a woman's skirt and see the baby floating around."

He smiled.

"I don't know what it would be like, but I imagine it as a warm place with light. I never see it as being dark. Dark is scary, and I can't think of a mother's womb as a scary place. The outside is where things get scary."

"Where do you think the light comes from?"

"I don't know. Maybe it filters from the outside in, or maybe it's the glow of the blood pumping from the mother's heart. But I know it has to be light."

"If the light reflects through the mother from the outside, then the outside can't be too scary."

"It doesn't have to be...no. It just is."

"Let's say a fetus is hibernating, until birth, then couldn't it be dark without be scary?"

"No. I don't believe that."

"Why not?"

"Because the light is warmth, reassurance."

"And the light of the outer world isn't as welcoming?"

"Leaving one's mother," her lower lip began to tremble, "leaving her body...that broken bond is tragic. I can't think of anything as sad."

"Even being held by her? Kissed, nursed?"

"Those are wonderful experiences, I'm sure, but..." Her voice cracked as she tried to clear her throat. "But no one can come between you in there. On the outside, the world puts its claim on you. A mother can't always be there." She swiped at her upper lip as her nose began to run.

He passed her a box of tissues.

"You are part of her and she is part of you. No one can separate that bond, unless she aborts..."

She cried now. "That was so sick..." She began rocking herself, holding her stomach. "They wrote that I had an abortion. I cou...I could never do that. I don't understand how anyone could."

"Then it's not even safe inside."

"Are you trying to confuse me?

"What is an ideal childhood, Marquel?"

She sniffed, looking up at him, tears standing in her eyes. "I think it would be having two warm, loving parents. Two people who care more about how their child feels, instead of thinking about what they can give him."

"What does the child feel?"

"Hurt, embarrassment. Sadness, happiness."

"Why do you put happiness last?"

"I don't really understand happiness."

His heart went out to her. "Go on."

"I think ideal parents would do things with their child. Coloring, fishing, swimming, playing. Non-material things."

"Are you a material person?"

"I appear to be."

"You're not sure?"

"I like the things I have. My house, my car. I can retreat into one and escape in the other."

"Anything else?"

"I don't understand...you're trying to confuse me."

"You said ideal parenting is non-materialistic, then implied that you are materialistic. Are you putting up a front?"

"I don't know!" She stood, grabbing for another cigarette and lighting it. She began to pace.

"Why are you uncomfortable now?" He was calm and at the same time fascinated by her mood swings. "You like what you have. What's wrong with that?"

"Listen, I can't think anymore. You've got me rattled. We were talking about kids, for Christ's sake..."

"The womb and the ideal parent."

"I don't want to discuss any of this now." The pitch of her voice rose. "My head's throbbing. I don't like this. I can't think."

"Do you need something for the headaches?"

"No. I don't like medication." She turned her back to him.

He smiled. It was refreshing to hear someone say they weren't interested in narcotics. He was looking into more holistic approaches for his practice.

"Our time is up." He stood.

She turned suddenly, her expression one of hurt. Lost. It was as though he had just slapped her face...was he throwing her out.

"Right." She picked up her cigarettes and purse and started for the door.

"Marquel?"

"Yes?" Her violet eyes looked into his.

"I hope I'll see you again."

"Perhaps."

He walked over to his desk and brought her a business card. "The emergency number is my residence. Call if you need to."

She didn't say anything, just slid the card into a pocket under her jersey and left.

CHAPTER FOURTEEN

It was Sunday. George knew he had plenty of time to make it to the nursing home. Traffic from Gulf Hammock to Tallahassee wasn't nearly as congested on the weekends. He usually sat around with the old man most of the afternoon and evening, watching football, leaving in time to get to work by eleven.

He steered the Bronco 4x4 onto U.S. Highway 19 and gave it some gas. The intersection had always given him the jitters. The accident. The accidents. Far too many lives had been taken at this spot. The unfortunate motorists, blinded by a clump of trees lining the median, approached the highway with a slow caution, forcing the 55 to 65 mile per hour traffic to deal with the vehicle immediately in its path. Too often there wasn't time to react. Once he was on the highway, George was himself again. It was just making that left turn...

He pushed the tape in, settling back with some country music. Alabama's "Old Flame" blared.

He sang along. "There's an old flame burning in your eye... that tears can't drown and makeup can't disguise..."

The lyrics pulled at his heartstrings. He couldn't help thinking of his sweet bride. He flipped the visor down and glanced at the picture of the two of them. Their honeymoon picture. Her hair had been cut in a pageboy back then. An ash-brown sheet of fine strands framed her plain, but handsome face. She never wore more than a hint of lip gloss. Make-up just wasn't her style.

They had gone to Disney World. It was all they could afford. His sister had given them the tickets as a wedding gift. Otherwise they wouldn't have had enough to make the trip at all.

His sister Margaret was just a year younger than George, but mature beyond her years, for as far back as he could remember. She'd work, save her money and travel for months at a time. Sometimes more than a year would go by before she contacted him. He wished she could be here now, going to see Pop. She could always cheer him up. But Margaret was a free spirit; no one tied her down. He could only wonder where she was and when she would show up again.

Their childhood had been fairly normal, growing up in Gulf Hammock. Their father, Harold Jennings, had worked in the quarry. Their mother, Laverne, had been a gardener and homemaker.

They had no more nor less than most children in the area. Laverne made all their play clothes and grew their vegetables. She bought their meats and staples in Chiefland, or the children and Harold would fish the Gulf of Mexico for fresh seafood. It was a happy time, a time George never wanted to forget and place he never wanted to leave.

CHAPTER FIFTEEN

"Marquel? Sophie. How are you dear? That's good. I was so disappointed we didn't get any photos of you at the party. Yes, I understand perfectly." Sophie was pure satin over the phone.

"I hate to cut this short, but I have guests and I really should...can I call you back?" Marquel lied. There was nobody at her house, save her housekeeper, Lawanda.

"Of course you can. Anyone I know?"

"No, I'm afraid not. Just some friends from out of town."

Lawanda grinned. The lean, black woman of twenty-three had a rich coffee and cream complexion, her voice a smooth, raspy alto, and her figure a petite size six. She was far too pretty to be a maid. Far too alluring to be kept from the public. She wanted to be a model.

Marquel suggested she change her name. But Lawanda was stubborn. She wanted to be somebody, on her own terms or not at all. And she wouldn't change her name. She was Lawanda Mae Jordan and nobody could take that away.

She cleared her throat. "Champagne. Over here?" She pointed absently, trying to give Marquel the opportunity to hang up quickly.

"Excuse me? Yes, I'll be there in a moment." Marquel smiled back at her.

"Let me make this quick," Sophie muttered. "Entertaining is serious business, I know."

Marquel rolled her eyes. She liked Sophie--she wasn't much of a snob--but Marquel didn't feel like wasting time on idle gossip.

"I'm on the committee with the Children's Hospital Benefit. Are you familiar?"

"Yes."

"Well, every year there's a telethon. You know, like Jerry's Kids? Ours is national also. And we're always looking for new talent."

"I'm afraid I don't understand."

"You're on a hot show, in the public eye..."

"But my character isn't one kids would know."

"We don't care about the kids...I didn't mean that...we're aiming for the adult donations."

"What could I do? Man a phone?"

"Well, perhaps, but..." The wheels were turning. Sophie wanted to do something different with the starlet. "The kids may be a good approach. I like it already. Say we have a reading... it would be good for your image, you know. Your character is slightly amoral."

"Reading?"

"Oh, let me think..." Sophie was having fun with the idea.

Lawanda motioned to Marquel. Marquel put her hand over the mouthpiece. "I know, I know...but I don't want to call her back."

"You're the star, honey. I wouldn't hold...I'd let my white housekeeper take a message."

They both laughed.

Sophie could hear the laughter. "Oh dear, your guests...I've got it, *The Velveteen Rabbit*!"

"The whole story?"

"Of course. I can arrange the time. We should be able to get a press release out in time for the kiddies to tune in..."

"You'll have to contact Ken."

"Is that necessary? This is charity."

"I'll do it as long as he okays it."

"How could he refuse? You'll be a smash...now back to your guests."

"My…? Yes. Thank you." Marquel hung up, turning to Lawanda. "She wants me to read *The Velveteen Rabbit* on the Children's Hospital Telethon."

"God. I can't read that one without having a nervous breakdown."

"It's a sad story?"

"Aren't they all?" She shook her head, starting to walk away. "They want to burn that poor bunny in the trash. No sir, I couldn't read that book again."

Evan gazed thoughtfully at Ken. "How was it?"

"Why do you ask?" Ken laughed softly. "You always ask, and my answer is always the same…I love everything about you, Ev."

Evan rolled on his side, propping his head against his hand. The taut brown muscles of his ever-tan body made his blonde hair appear almost white. They could almost be mistaken for brothers, with the same brilliant blue eyes and blonde hair. The only difference was Evan's locks were natural, while Ken's came from a bottle. Evan's tight curls were beginning to grow out, framing his square face with a soft glow. Ken's face was an inverted triangle.

They had been lovers for more than three years. Each led a separate life, though more often than not they were together—wrapped in each other's arms, kissing, caressing, and playing.

Evan ran a finger over Ken's flat stomach, which Ken caught and brought up to his mouth, kissing it. "Maybe we should move in together again. Settle down."

"Maybe, in another year," Evan answered. "How's our girl?"

"She's been to a shrink."

"And?"

Ken sat up. "It's done her some good. I believe that much. I met with her doctor at the Polo Lounge. What soulful eyes… you'd love him…Anyway, she seems more relaxed."

"Poor kid," Evan sighed. Rolling over on his back, he put his hands behind his hand. "She was so green when she got here. I feel like she's our little girl."

"She's not much younger than us."

"In her heart she is…you know that."

Ken nodded.

"I can't tell you how much I felt for her the day you brought her here." Evan had a luxurious home at the Colony, Malibu's hideaway for the stars. His neighbors included Martin Sheen, Cher, and Larry Hagman, among others. Evan had made a small fortune in his late twenties as a record executive.

At thirty-five, he found no reason to do anything more than relax and semi-retire. His company, OffBeat, was earning him a handsome income. He could afford to play at leisure. He had met Ken at a friend's party, a low-key event with a handful of people spinning some Donna Summer albums and smoking a little grass. Ken had no idea of Evan's wealth then. Evan had dearly loved Ken's enthusiasm, impatience and naïve business sense.

They had grown closer over the years, but Evan still wasn't ready for a long-term commitment. Ken had a growing business. It wasn't fair to ask him to leave all that behind to travel.

"Why don't you bring Marquel up next weekend? I'd love for the three of us to get together again."

"Ev...I think I should keep some distance. I don't want her thinking I'm keeping tabs on her."

"Then I'll call her. We'll take the boat out, then dinner at La Scala. Why not?"

"Why not?" Ken smiled falsely. He could see that in agreeing he had pleased Evan. But he didn't necessarily want to share him, not now. Not when things seemed perfect.

"Come here."

Ken nuzzled in. "You know I love you."

"I know, shhh," Evan whispered. "Wouldn't it be great if we could have a kid, adopt one? We'd be great parents."

Ken laughed. "Yeah, I'd be pulling my hair out while you stood back amused."

"That's what I mean. It would be beautiful. I could see us with a little girl. Little girls need daddies."

"What about a boy?"

"I don't know...boys are different. They're rough, and abrupt."

"And little girls are sassy know-it-alls."

"Like you. Just like Daddy Ken."

Ken stirred a little, resting his head on Evan's chest. He could hear his heartbeat, feel the heat of his body. He closed his eyes. This was heaven, right here, in this bed.

Jackie stood beside Marnie in front of the girls' bathroom mirror. Marnie applied a second coat of plum pink lipstick to her full bow lips.

"You gonna go to Rick's party?" Jackie asked.

"Hmmm." Marnie rubbed her lips together, pouting at her reflection. She was the school beauty...a medium built, full-breasted, fourteen-year-old trapped in the body of a legal adult. Her thick black hair was always impeccably styled in a ponytail or spritzed up to add inches to her height. Her sultry green eyes gave her hair the richness of black velvet. "Rick is a geek. No way."

"He may be a geek, but he's a lot more fun than Johnny and Derek. Remember his camcorder party? Everybody brought their own, and like filmed different segments of the party. It was awesome." Jackie began to laugh. "They caught Derek taking a piss."

"*Dis*-gusting!" Marnie put her lipstick back in her purse.

"Yeah, but Derek was so wasted, he didn't even know until he saw the tape."

Marnie laughed. "That I would have liked to see."

"Marnie?"

"Yeah..." She turned to Jackie, who had stopped laughing for the moment.

"There's something I want to tell you, but you have to absolutely swear not to tell anyone..."

Marnie's expression was indignant.

"I know I can trust you," Jackie tried again, "it's just that this is a major secret, about one of my father's patients. Not only would he shit if he knew I told anyone, but he would probably get in big trouble too."

"Is that all? One of your dad's patients?" Marnie turned back to the mirror. He doesn't have anything worth talking about, Jackie."

"You'll change your mind when you hear this."

"Try me."

"You have to promise me first. You can't even tell your mom and dad. Your dad would leak it to the trades so fast…"

"If you don't think you can trust me, don't tell me. As for my dad, leave him out. Is that what your mom and dad say about my dad? My parents think…"

"Forget it." Jackie scooped her books off the counter, folding her arms around them. "All right, I won't tell you." She walked toward the door. Marnie had been a good friend, but sometimes she acted too superior for her own good. Her dad had a big mouth; everyone knew.

Marnie's sigh was marked with disgust. "Okay, I promise."

"Forget it." Jackie paused, her back to the girl, smiling in satisfaction. "Rick is uncool, my dad's a bore, my parents are creeps. Sorry I bothered."

Marnie followed Jackie out of the bathroom, picking up her pace to walk beside Jackie as they made their way down the hall. The bell rang. Marnie looked pleadingly at Jackie.

"Okay, okay," Jackie said.

"You called my dad a traitor."

"We don't have time for this. You hurt my feelings."

"You hurt mine."

"Let's forget it."

"Marquel is my dad's new patient."

"No *way!*"

Jackie knew Marnie believed her. "Way."

"Radical."

"See?"

"You gonna meet her?"

"Uh…yeah. But not for a while."

"Let me know, I wanna be there."

"We'll see."

"Your secret's safe with me, Jack."

"I gotta go. Old Man Ferrister's gonna scream if I'm late again."

"See ya lunch period."

"Okay." Jackie broke into a run, her pink LA Gear sneakers squeaking behind her.

CHAPTER SIXTEEN

George's ears perked. He heard a faint rustling just beyond the cypress stump, not more than ten feet ahead. It was cool this morning, cooler than it had been at the opening of hunting season. He could see the buck's full rack between a clump of branches and oak leaves. The animal was aware of him.

He took another step forward. Twigs and dry leaves crackled under his snakeskin boots. The buck leaped to his left. He pulled the rifle around. The buck was directly in sight, then sprang north. He fired at the animal once, twice, realizing that he would have to track him deeper into the woods.

It was the damnedest thing, he thought, as he shook his head. How you could be so close to an animal and still miss him? He pointed the gun down and walked toward the trail he'd cut some ten years earlier. This was his entertainment, hunting, fishing and just being in the great outdoors. During season, he'd hunt after work, and then go home to shower and sleep, getting up in time to eat before he left for work again. He'd stopped watching television. He didn't even own a VCR. Occasionally, he would rent one at the Bob's General Store. *Batman* was his favorite. He remembered the series from when he was a kid. He couldn't seem to get enough of the comics.

His dad had raised him and Margaret on super heroes. Harold believed every kid needed a hero. Their mother had died of cancer when George was fifteen and Margaret was fourteen.

They couldn't bear to keep up her garden after she passed away. Instead, they picked vegetables at local farms or bought their groceries in town.

George learned diesel mechanics while still in high school. His father's closest friend had taken him under his wing and taught him everything he knew. It was an honest living for a young man. It kept him fed and clothed.

The air was fragrant with the scent of pine. Hunting was his passion. It wasn't so much the act, but the sport that intrigued him. He froze for a moment; off in the distance he could hear men. He knew they had spotted the buck. He called to them, identifying his location so they wouldn't mistake his movement for the animal's.

"I think you nipped him," a voice called. "There's a trail of blood. We'll follow it. Thanks."

George didn't answer; instead, he followed in the same general direction as the voices. He could see one of the men carrying a semi-automatic weapon. *Not very sportsmanlike in his estimation.*

George was getting further and further away from the actual hunt. He wanted to spend more time outdoors, just being out. He'd considered buying a fishing boat and cruising the Wacassassa, maybe even venturing into the Gulf.

The sound of a pig snuffling around in the underbrush caught his attention. The black and white patched animal was huge and had four little piglets following closely behind. He couldn't help thinking how cute the little guys were.

A lump rose in his throat. He once knew a little girl who dearly loved small animals. He would capture baby hares, turtles and owls for her. It had been a lifetime ago when things were simpler and love was unconditional. He still loved her he believed more than he ever had.

He stepped aside as the sow and her brood scurried by. His heart in his mouth, he reached down and patted the last piglet as it squealed past. He could feel his heart ache as it had the last time he saw the little girl. The very last time…

CHAPTER SEVENTEEN

Zach let his receptionist show Marquel in. It was only their second session, but he had allotted her more time, keeping his entire afternoon open.

"Please, have a seat." He sat after she did. "I'd like to throw an idea at you."

She looked radiant in a soft cotton-knit jumpsuit. The peach and olive tones gave her a spring fresh appearance.

"Anything." She smiled.

He hoped her self-assurance wouldn't fade when he made his suggestion. Guilt was already beginning to creep up on him. "I'd like to audio tape the rest of our sessions. I think it will help me to help you."

Her smile settled to a straight line. "I see."

"These tapes would remain in my possession, strictly confidential. Unless you object...?"

"Is this necessary?"

"That's hard to say. In having them available, I would be able to review them, to assess your progress, and..."

"Progress."

"Of course," he watched her settle back against the couch, "if I'm unable to help you, I will refer you to another doctor."

"Specializing in nut cases? Split personalities?" She laughed bitterly.

"Specializing in an area of psychiatry or psychology that would be most beneficial to your needs." He felt instantly that he'd insulted her. He was more apprehensive about taping the sessions.

"If I become uncomfortable, will you cut the machine off?"

"Certainly."

"All right." She dug through her purse coming up with her cigarettes and a lighter.

"Shall we begin?"

She nodded, holding the lighter to the cigarette and inhaling deeply. She resembled a modern-day Harlow in full curls of platinum. Peach became her, matching the faint hues in her cheeks and her long, slender neck. She wore a delicate gold chain and cross.

"I see you're wearing a cross. We haven't discussed religion. Would you like to begin there?"

She looked down at the tiny icon, rubbing it between her thumb and index finger. "Oh this? Evan gave it to me. I stayed with him when I first came to Los Angeles Sometimes I still house-sit for him when he's in Europe. He's a friend of Ken's."

Zach wondered how it was possible to feel jealous of a man he did not know. Evan. Why did he feel so for a woman he barely knew? She had meant enough to Evan for him to give her an expensive symbolic gift. "It holds no religious value for you?"

"No, I wish it did." She turned away, exhaling smoke. "I don't believe in God. It's not that I don't want to, it's just that I'm numb to religion. I don't know who to pray to, or for what. Does God giveth and taketh away such things as sanity?"

"Wearing a cross doesn't make you feel…mocking?"

"The man who gave it to me has religious convictions. He meant well toward me. It would be an insult for me not to accept his gift, the intent he offered."

"This man means a great deal to you?"

"Yes. Along with Ken, he's responsible for my career. They're the only friends I have here."

"You weren't sure of your friends in our first session. Why didn't you mention Ken and…Evan?"

"Maybe I didn't feel like trusting you."

He took the statement to mean she was opening to him, beginning to trust. Were she not a patient, he'd have asked her out the moment he laid eyes on her.

"What is it about Evan that you trust?"

"He's down to earth, not on edge, like Ken. I trust Ken, but not in the same way."

Zach understood this. His lunch with Ken remained fresh in his mind. It wasn't that the man seemed totally false, but he sensed something about him that would make complete trust impossible.

Unfortunately for Zach, the Polo Lounge had been crowded. Ken had found it difficult to concentrate; he was too busy trying to eavesdrop on nearby tables. He swore he heard a deal being made at the next table, explaining that it was rumored that the author Hilary Smithfield was in town with her agent, pitching her latest historical epic. Ken had asked Zach to lean in and see if he could catch anything. Hilary was said to be a beast—no photos were ever printed on her book jackets.

Ken knew enough that producer Carl Shimburg was dining with an unidentified man and woman; he was certain the pair were Hilary, and Mauri Gross, her agent.

Zach stood, intending to leave. Would Ken ever make his point? The man begged him to sit, which he did, grudgingly. Ken proceeded to tell him about Marquel's ineptitude while keeping one ear perked ninety degrees to the left.

"Evan is someone you feel you could call on if distressed?" Zach asked Marquel.

"No."

"I'm sorry, I don't understand." His gaze wandered to the cross at her throat again.

"What I meant was that he's really Ken's friend. If I needed him, I'm sure he would probably help me...I just wouldn't want to burden him, after what he's done for me."

"Then the gift wasn't one of an intimate nature?"

She laughed. "I think he felt sorry for me."

"Would you, as you put it, burden your lover with your problems?"

"No…sometimes I talk to Ken, but he has an investment in me. I owe him. I must let him know if there's something…I have no privacy, no life, I'm here talking with you, but that is because it's your job to listen."

Zach watched as her head sank into her hands. His heart went out to her once more…would he be able to help her? Not unless he stopped wanting her. This silent admission shocked him. "Marquel, would you like to take a break?"

She raised her head, brushing the back of her hand across her mouth. "No, I'm okay. It's just…sometimes I realize how alone I am. I should be…right? No one deserves to be dragged into this…" Her gaze grew distant, trance-like for a moment. And just like that, she snapped out of it, reaching habitually for her cigarettes.

"Do you feel a lover can have an investment in a person? Like an agent…"

"Only the love they feel for that person."

"That's all we really have sometimes, isn't it? Our feelings?" Zach wondered aloud.

For the first time, Marquel looked at Dr. Zach Manning as a man, not a doctor. He surely had a life, a family, his own personal discontents. She wanted to know what he was thinking, what made him digress from his questioning.

"The time spent on a relationship, isn't that an investment?"

Did he realize how vulnerable he seemed? Marquel wondered. Maybe it was just her emotions—getting wrapped up in the questioning. It was as if he asked the last question to reassure himself. "Time is an investment," she agreed, "but it isn't the same. If one or the other falls out of love…if something goes wrong…that person isn't obligated to stay because of time spent."

"Why?"

"Because…it just doesn't have to be that way."

"So, you escape?"

"I didn't say that."

"Didn't you?"

"No, I didn't."

"Then I misunderstood," he broke off. Where was this conversation going?

"What if children are involved in the relationship?"

"I wouldn't know."

"Hypothetically speaking."

"I don't know. Would you stay in a destructive relationship for a child's sake?" She stared at him half expecting him to answer. He didn't. She was getting angry. "I forgot, you get to ask all the questions. I'm the one being dissected."

"What would you leave behind, the child or the relationship? This is for your benefit, Marquel."

"I told you before, I wouldn't know."

"Hypothetically."

She didn't feel like answering.

"I'm sorry. Shall we get back to religion?"

They talked the entire afternoon. He stopped the recorder after the first tape ran out and didn't bother to begin another. Before long they were both seated on the couch, sharing ideas and theories about God. He found her to be extremely open. Comfortable. It wasn't a bad experience for him either—to stop playing doctor and getting to know one another. Though he'd quit smoking years before, he bummed one from her. She laughed when he almost choked on the first drag.

She didn't want the day to end and it surprised him when she suggested they meet outside the office for her next session. She'd long stopped thinking of him as her doctor in the waning hours. She suspected if they met at the ocean for a walk and talk she would be able to tell him more—to learn more from him. She wanted his support, and he had agreed to meet with her for this...*alternative* therapy.

Zach returned to his condo with great anticipation. He hadn't felt this young or close to anyone in years. The mirror reflected his feelings—he brushed his hands over his hair, assessing his clothes. He needed to be more casual, maybe buy some new things before next week. What the hell, he hadn't bought himself anything in years. In fact, he rarely wore anything that didn't require dry cleaning with the exception of his socks and underwear. He could use the change.

Jackie had called earlier, eager to hear about Marquel. It was odd how often he had to remind himself of confidentiality. He had to resist the urge of talking about his sympathy for the actress or his attraction to her. God knew he'd already overstepped his boundaries. For the life of him, he couldn't remember when it had happened, or if she'd stepped over the line the first time she entered his office. For Jackie's sake, he acknowledged having seen Marquel and admitted that she was continuing with regular sessions.

He made himself a microwave dinner of Fettuccine Alfredo and a couple of glasses of rosé. He was relaxed and decided to watch some television, but nothing seemed to hold his interest. He was restless with the thought of her.

When he closed his eyes, he could see her standing before him. Her peach complexion, the sheer apricot lipstick and soft olive eye shadow gave her a haunting appeal. His vision of her changed as he dozed off. Her eyes were misty with passion, taunting him. Her smile turned sultry and alluring as she whispered longingly to him. By one in the morning, he'd decided to take a cold shower. By three, he'd gotten up to drink a couple more glasses of wine. He couldn't remember when he fell asleep, but the next morning when his alarm went off at six-thirty, he awoke to a splitting headache.

Wine had always had that effect on him. To top it off, the lack of sleep, combined with Mimi Ledbetter's usual Wednesday morning session, insured a bona fide migraine. He called his receptionist and had her reschedule the woman—something he hadn't done in years. She would moan and bitch the next time he saw her, but he just couldn't bear the thought of her Brooklyn dialect pounding the hangover into his eardrums and temples.

CHAPTER EIGHTEEN

"Gas her up," Collins told the station attendant. He'd traveled the course of several days trying to trace Marquel's journey of fame from Florida to California. He was getting nowhere fast.

The roommate in Jupiter did remember Marquel had traveled from Gainesville, after he'd offered her a hundred dollars. She said Marquel had told her she had an apartment in the college town just before arriving on the state's east coast.

He'd checked with the University of Florida and Florida State to see if she had attended or graduated either school. No one had a Marquel Chapman on record. He checked phone directories and called every Chapman from Tallahassee to Jacksonville and not one of them had the faintest idea what he was talking about. Hearing the first name, of course, they wanted to stay on the line and question him. He couldn't call Gilman until he had something. He'd yet to take the final steps, checking the public records, marriage licenses or police records.

He looked across the street at the truck stop. His stomach ached for something other than another fast food burger. "How's the food?" he nodded to the attendant.

"I don't think ya'd fit in. Them's good ol' boys over there. Theyn't take kindly to city folks."

"What about college kids?"

"College," he laughed, "them kids don't eat there. They got their own territory about three miles up a spell."

Collins rolled his eyes. He could barely tolerate the man's slow talk, much less his opinion of where one should dine. He wouldn't bother with the truck stop. He'd take the rental car and drive to the nearest airport and get the hell out of Florida. It had been an aggravating experience, one he could always embellish on, but nevertheless, he had to know more. She was getting into his blood.

He didn't like a story he couldn't crack. He had no intention of letting hers slide by.

CHAPTER NINETEEN

Jackie stormed back and forth in the kitchen as her father sat on a bar stool, his chin supported by the heel of his palm. He was amused by her tirade.

"Daddy, I know if you really wanted to, you'd find a way for me to meet her."

"Oh? And how is that?" He couldn't tell her about the session wherein they drove up the Pacific Coast Highway until they found a spot to their liking. He couldn't explain that they'd walked the beach and drew pictures in the sand.

They had behaved like two children and it was becoming more apparent that Marquel was feeling the same stirring for him as he felt for her. He'd wanted to ask her to dinner, but managed to keep his distance, agreeing instead to meet her for a Sunday drive and a picnic at Will Rogers State Park. Jackie would be livid if she knew next week, while she and Marnie were sunning at the beach, he and Marquel would be together…not so many miles away.

"You don't care, Daddy. You're not even listening."

"I am listening. I just don't have a response for you."

"Ooh!" She stamped her foot to punctuate the utterance. Her ash-blonde hair bounded up in her banana clip. "Marnie's…I mean…"

His eyes narrowed on her. "Marnie's what? Did you tell her?"

"No," she lied. Her cheeks grew hot under his scrutiny and she turned to the refrigerator. "I'm thirsty. All this pleading is making my throat dry." She secretly hoped he would allow her to drop the subject. "Do you want anything?"

"No." He continued glaring at her. He wanted to display trust rather than openly accusing her, even though he knew damn well she was lying. He was concerned for Marquel's sake. "Jackie, I'm going to trust that you haven't said anything to Marnie or your friends. You know the rules, honey. You're like a politician's, military or attorney's child; we have to respect family business. Our children understand the serious nature of privacy. It's my fault I slipped. But I won't go over it…you understand."

"You want me to make breakfast for us tomorrow?" Jackie peered over her Coke can. She always enjoyed a big Sunday breakfast with pancakes and omelets and fresh fruit. Boy, did she feel guilty!

He laughed. "You're bribing me with breakfast? Since when do you get up first?"

"I will. If you want, I mean."

"What if I call your bluff, little lady? You'll be up to your elbows in pancake batter."

"Ha ha."

"You're on."

"You'll be surprised…I'm not a bad cook."

"I'd like to know where you learned. Carmen certainly won't let you touch anything in her kitchen other than the microwave."

"I've been watching her. This may come as a surprise to you, but I *can* read."

"Okay. I'll get up when the smoke alarm goes off."

She mimicked him, poking her tongue out at him.

He smiled at his pride and joy and secretly wondered how much she had said. He loved her and didn't want to start a guilt trip. It was his own damn fault he had relaxed his mouth!

Marquel was anxious to see Zach. Her sessions, she thought, were more like visits among old friends. She knew she was falling for him and what had been a struggle for identity no longer seemed important. Maybe her past was not to be remembered. She had Zach now and it was evident he felt that same for her. They shared so much in the short time they'd known one another— fears, hopes, dreams. He'd briefly mentioned his ex-wife and she knew he had a daughter in her early teens. She was anxious to meet the girl. She envisioned her having the same deep, dark eyes as her father, with a rich Mediterranean complexion like his.

Their day at the ocean had been so peaceful and pleasant that Marquel knew this picnic would be much the same. It was soothing to be near him, looking into his dark eyes and seeing the traces of longing in them. Sometimes they wouldn't speak at all.

When he picked her up that afternoon, bearing an oversized basket with cold meats, cheeses, bread and wine, she felt like kissing him. She restrained herself from doing so, for fear passion might abort the picnic altogether.

He looked like a boy carrying goods to his grandmother. He was handsomely attired in khaki slacks, a crisp white button-down shirt with the sleeves rolled up. The scent of his woodsy cologne had her lingering in his essence. She had chosen white slacks and a pullover sleeveless sweater patterned in an intricate Navajo print of turquoise, mauve and gray. She slipped into a pair of white canvas Candies as they walked out the door.

They drove through Will Rogers State Historical Park looking for just the spot. Towering redwoods and pines shaded the lush greenery. They found a quiet spot sunny enough to keep the cool autumn breezes from cutting through them.

She was almost too excited, much too nervous to eat, and suggested they walk some of the trails and take in the marvelous view. He agreed. As they walked hand in hand she felt for the first time like everything was going to be all right. Each time he squeezed her hand, she could feel warmth coursing through her. She never wanted him to let go. When she looked into his eyes, she could see a desire that matched her own.

The rest of the day drifted by lazily. They spoke very little—there was no need. Their hearts created the dialogue of the moment.

She could not think of a single person she'd known who would court her in such a fashion. He was gentlemanly in his ways and she adored these qualities more with each passing moment.

After several hours lounging on the blanket, watching the clouds through the towering redwoods and discussing their puffy white formations, they decided it was time to move on.

Neither suggested where they might go. She hated for the day to end. She loved listening to his voice as he spoke with adoration of his daughter, Jackie, about how intelligent and comical the girl was. It was obvious the child was the most important person in his life.

Marquel was relieved he wasn't seeing anyone. She told him there was no one special in her life. She had dated a few actors, dined somewhat regularly at Spago for publicity's sake and had been escorted to art shows and theater engagements, but none of these dates captured her interest. Everything became an appearance—a way of staying in and not stepping on any toes. She'd had a brief affair with a twenty-year-old newcomer and he'd been smitten with her, but he bored her. She just didn't feel like making an effort. He had been away from home for the first time and seemed to need someone to cling to. She couldn't be his mother and his lover, so she dropped him and stopped dating shortly thereafter.

"Would you like a drink?" Zach had asked her twice. She was too busy looking around his apartment, noticing the decorator touches that failed to capture his personality. The living room was hard and elegant, in glossy black and gray tones. The furniture seemed to stare at you. The bedrooms were less intimidating—the master was in beige and blue with indigo focal points. Not quite warm or inviting, but she could see him there, sleeping, whispering to her...

"No thank you, I'm fine."

"Too much wine?"

"I've met my quota."

"I know what you mean. How about a Perrier?"

"That sounds good."

"I'll be right back." He returned with two glasses.

She sipped at her mineral water disinterestedly. He smiled, watching her. He moved closer. "May I kiss you?"

She wasn't surprised; instead, she was pleased he had asked. Taking her into his arms, their first kiss was sweet, soft.

Their desire seemed to mutually taunt them, making it difficult to quench their ardor and impossible to break the embrace. She took his hand and led him to the bedroom.

He laid her down, covering her heated body with his own. They struggled with each other's clothing for what seemed like an eternity before their flesh met. He made love to her with a passion born of vice, and again and again with the gentleness of a poet.

CHAPTER TWENTY

He sat up against the pillows, staring at her sleeping figure. He felt more alive than he had in years. She was nestled close to his waist, stirring at his change of position. In the drowsiness of sleep, she raised up slightly, wrapping her arm about his waist and resting her warm cheek against the flat of his stomach. He held his breath, resting a hand on her shoulder.

He didn't want to wake her, but the sensation of having her reach out for him was overwhelming, beyond anything he'd felt before. He knew he was at least twenty years older than this luscious creature wrapped around him. No matter her age or temperament, he felt blessed by her presence.

He leaned forward, stroking the platinum curtain of curls flowing down her neck. It was all too good to be true, the way they fell into this, fully aware and hand in hand. And yet she was still his patient, still in need of help and haunted by her illness. His only concern at this moment was to assist her in overcoming this nightmare.

He moved down beside her, cradling her in his arms. With a feather touch he kissed her hair, nuzzling himself in close to spoon her back. Her skin felt good against his chest. He felt he could stay here forever, just listening to the even rhythm of her breathing.

If only he could figure out what demons she wrestled with, what event or series of events robbed her of her true identity, the self she was born to. He had seen adults who had been abused as children reach a mid-life crisis in which they escaped into child-hood fantasy characters, personalities they had taken on belatedly to hide from the torment a parent had put them through.

As he tried to imagine what Marquel's personal torment was, he envisioned her as a child, her small frame perfect, fine hair bouncing, slightly chubby hands covering her mouth as she giggled, those lavender-blue eyes crinkling. A lump rose in his throat. How could anyone harm such a precious creature? He couldn't understand such behavior. But then he knew that many abusers grew up abused themselves.

He couldn't see that happening with Marquel. Even had she been abused, he didn't believe her capable of abuse. No. She cherished the thought of having a child.

Abuse was very possibly an element of her past. As fragile as she was, he realized, this relationship could break her if things didn't work out…He just couldn't see hurting her. He also couldn't see himself sleeping through another night without her beside him. Should her mental state deteriorate to the point of being institutionalized, he felt sure he would follow. She was in his heart now, perhaps since the moment he laid eyes on her.

He swallowed hard. Part of him wanted to wake her up, to tell her he was falling in love with her. But he restrained the urge, telling himself he might not be able to help her professionally. His body grew rigid, fighting the passion that ran through him; the pain was a pleasure in itself. Tears flooded his eyes as she stirred. She sensed his shift of emotion. He rubbed her shoulder comfortingly, soothing her. She sighed, relaxing once more in his arms. Loving her would be dangerous for them both. But not loving her would be a crime.

He closed his eyes, tears stinging out. He would stand by her, no matter what happened.

CHAPTER TWENTY-ONE

The host, a toothy blonde actor from an overrated sitcom, had taken his cue from the commercial cutaway. They were back on the air, the phone lines open, and the telethon was well into its twelfth hour. Marquel was given a five-minute cue on sound stage two. The host would then cut to her.

The stage was designed to look like a child's bedroom with giant toys that dwarfed the size of the actress. She was given an entire half hour with one five-minute break to read an abridged version of *The Velveteen Rabbit*. She positioned herself on a large pastel building block and closed her eyes, trying to relax.

The floor director called a one-minute cue, which made her more nervous. She had never performed before a live television audience, much less a live audience of children. The show had begun at eight o'clock the night before and it was now eight o'clock on Sunday morning. VCRs were being set and some restless children were no doubt tuning in to hear this wonderful story told by a beautiful porcelain doll, the actress Marquel. Most parents knew her from the soap opera that came on too late for their children to watch.

"And five, four, three, two..." The floor director pointed to her.

She froze for a moment then seemed to go on automatic. She introduced herself, straightened the folds of the white pinafore covering her flower print dress. She opened the book and began to read.

On a monitor the pages of the story would flash across the screen, then cut back to the actress. She really enjoyed the story as they first introduced the boy and his new Christmas toys.

It was going so smoothly that she was able to block out the camera crew and the fact she was reading to a live viewing audience estimated to be somewhere in the seven-figure range. Her expressions were animated and as genuine as the enchanted words of Margery Williams. It was going very well, and the time seemed to move quickly. She became a little flustered at the five-minute cue. Soon they would break for a commercial, and then return for the story's conclusion.

The story was divided at the point where the Velveteen Rabbit meets real rabbits for the first time, just before it is learned that the little boy had become very ill. Marquel stumbled gingerly as she announced the commercial break.

She sighed, biting her quivering lip. Lawanda was right; she never would've agreed to read the story had she known how sad it was. It was choking her up. The boy and the bunny would soon be separated, never to see one another again but for a brief instance in the woods. The rabbit's very existence was threatened before he would have a chance to be made "Real"—and there was the real teardrop that falls from his eye! The camera and stage crew were merely shadows in the distance. She fought for composure.

"The phone lines are mad with callers…"

"God, do you believe the emotion she's putting…"

"She's a smash…"

"Close up on camera two…"

"What acting…"

She vaguely wondered who was speaking. She could hear the words through her earpiece. They seemed to float on the air, but they couldn't filter through her sadness. She blinked at the mist in her eyes.

"Okay and…take it!"

The floor director looked alternately from her to the monitor. The camera, thank God, wasn't picking up the trembling of her hands as she turned the pages. The massive set and numerous close-ups made it impossible to notice.

"The kiddies across the nation are crying with her, I've even heard the president is going to call. Can you believe this shit?" The host laughed under his breath. "*Entertainment Tonight* is going to air a segment and they're trying to line up an interview with her agent now. All that for sobbing over a kid's fairy tale."

The floor director signaled her to wrap it up, they were about to run over.

When she was finally off the air, she threw herself on a big pink bear and sobbed.

The crew stood around mumbling. They hadn't known quite what to expect, but they had to get her off the set fast. They were expected to strike the Pat Walker Show before they left.

"We gotta break everything down, lady," one man approached her. "I'm sorry." He didn't know what for; this was probably her usual release after a performance.

She sat up and stared at him. Her eyes were red and bore an expression of anguish. She didn't say a word, just stood, untied the pinafore and then stormed off.

Jackie woke her father with a panicked tug at his arm. "Wake up…wake up, it's on!"

"What?" Zach rolled over, looking up at the girl.

"The telethon," she said. "Marquel's on."

He pulled himself up. "Oh."

"Daddy!"

"I'm awake!"

"Hurry."

"All right, all right." He slipped his feet into the battered slippers at his beside and padded down the hallway after his daughter.

Plopped on the sofa in an old flannel gown, Jackie hit the remote control, turning up the volume. Marquel was already reading the story and Zach grinned. She looked beautiful. *Heidi grown up,* he thought. Her reading had begun smoothly. He knew how nervous she was about the engagement.

Looking at her now, he found it hard to believe she had made such a fuss about it. The camera loved her.

"I love this story, don't you Daddy?"

"I don't think I've heard it," he answered absently.

"Then listen, I'll be quiet."

He nodded, leaning forward and clasped his hands together, resting his elbows on his knees.

He wasn't listening to the story, just watching her. Watching the beautiful doll perched on a pastel alphabet block. He couldn't wait to call her and congratulate her.

Her velvet, raspy voice pitched high for emphasis as the illustrations of William Nicholson flashed on the screen. He was now beginning to understand the story.

Her voice sounded somewhat stressed when she announced the commercial. He wondered how she would do when they came back. Jackie had already informed him that the story got much sadder.

The commercial break ended. Marquel began to read again.

Zach's eyes grew wide. He could tell she was struggling as they did a closeup. The familiar glazed expression that had always eluded him was back. Somewhere inside her, there were threads coming loose, unraveling. Would he be able to knit them back before this fragile woman fell apart? She was crying now and his eyes watered. Crying about a little rabbit, forced to leave the boy he loved and become real in the bargain. He pinched back the tickling sensation in his nose.

"Daddy, you're crying," Jackie sniffled, her eyes brimming with tears.

"It's okay." He hugged her.

"It's so sad," she quavered.

He nodded, keeping his eyes on the screen. The sadness in Marquel's expression was overwhelming. He felt hopeless, like there was no end to her torture. It was as though in loving her he had become part of her, but he still couldn't understand the root of her anguish. How much more desperate she must feel if he could feel it too.

Her voice broke as she read the final lines, where the bunny, now real, is glimpsed by the boy. And the boy doesn't know that the real bunny is his old toy bunny who is now living a new different life.

Joyce wanted Ty Mayo's undivided attention.

She moved toward his chair, squatted beside him and rested her massive breast over his right arm. "You know you make me crazy," she lied.

He grinned.

"Let's not mince words, let's get down to business."

"Business?" His mind was racing.

"Uh huh."

"The only unfinished business I see is a beautiful woman in need of a little Mayo."

She laughed throatily.

"Anything."

"What's the future hold for *Suburban Life*?"

"At least five to seven…season run…" He grabbed at her.

She pushed him back. "Spin-offs, Ty…are you developing a new series?"

She didn't seem the slightest bit aroused by his obsessive staring and grabbing.

"Well, Joyce…I love your tits."

"Enough to give them a series of their own?" She knew she could ask for anything at this moment…

CHAPTER TWENTY-TWO

Zach strode past Carnie and Sam on his way to Marquel's dressing room. They had become accustomed to his frequent visits. The doctor was now a permanent fixture in the *Suburban Life* family, as permanent as fixtures got in this business.

Sid liked Zach a lot. Too much. He couldn't seem to get enough information and free consultations.

Any ache or pain that flared up during a shoot, Sid wouldn't hesitate to ask Zach. In fact, the hypochondria seemed to spread like wildfire. Joyce had a chest cold, wanted a private physical in her dressing room. And Sam asked him to analyze his dreams. Zach promptly referred Sam to a psychic that he'd wanted to "pay back." The phony had been close to Isabel, advising her on the divorce proceedings and tried to swindle him with numerous bills for services she claimed were rendered while the couple was still married. The rest he encouraged to consult their regular physicians.

He walked into her dressing room.

Marquel, bathed in the soft lights surrounding her make-up mirror, caught his reflection and smiled back at him. The room was small and cozy like a child's bedroom. Just enough space to spread out, but for no more than a few hours.

She watched him in her mirror addressing him with a smile. She had taken off most of her makeup, appearing fresh and devoid of the falseness that surrounded show business.

"Hi," he said, placing a hand on either of her shoulders. "Tired?"

"Never too tired for you."

He kissed her hair.

"Then why don't we go back to my place? There's something I'd like to discuss with you."

"Discuss?" she smiled. "Are we really going to waste time talking?

"Nah."

"I didn't think so."

"I'm crazy about you, you know that?"

Her lips teased another smile, "No. Why don't you tell me about it?"

He pulled up a chair and spun hers around to face him. "No joking. I have something to say."

"What is it?

"I just bought a house."

Her brows knitted. "Where?"

"In Beverly Hills."

"But why?"

"I'm giving up the condo. It's too confining and, also...I promised Jackie."

"Oh."

"But that isn't my point," he cleared his throat. "I would like for you to move in. I want us to spend more time together."

"What about Jackie? We haven't even met. Does she know about us?"

"I have Jackie every other weekend, and I'm sure the two of you will do fine. She's been dying to meet you." He took both her hands. "Does the idea of Jackie staying with us bother you?"

"I didn't agree to move in with you, Zach. Have you considered the possibility that Jackie may dislike the arrangement?"

"Please say you will."

She fought to say the right thing. "I don't know..."

"You can decorate the place however you want. If you want designer everything or Herculon, it doesn't matter. As long as we're together." He was smiling big.

She had never seen him so happy. "What about Jackie?"

"I'd like to get the two of you together…in advance if I can."
A flash of professionalism hit him. He shouldn't be pressuring
her. Were his emotions ruling again?

"I'm all for that," she sighed. She would never treat Jackie
badly… "Why do you look concerned now, Zach. I'll move in
with you."

He crushed her against him in an ecstatic hug. "I was worried
that I was pushing you."

CHAPTER TWENTY-THREE

Jackie loved the house.

The four-bedroom four-bath home built in the early twenties was scheduled for a "tear down." The property was more valuable than the home, but Zach was growing fond of the old structure and its sturdy foundation. Hell, he didn't want to rebuild. It may be the thing to do, but he didn't necessarily agree with the Realtor.

The home had once belonged to silent film idol Sally Sweet. A swimming pool had since been added, along with a guesthouse just beyond the tennis court. But the teenager found the balcony overlooking the garden from the bedroom she'd picked for herself more appealing.

She later informed her father that he could have the largest of the four bedrooms facing the entrance gates.

"Thank you, sweetheart." Zach couldn't have been happier with his daughter's enthusiasm. In fact, he'd left her in charge of selecting the furniture and arcade games for the great room.

He stood by as she surveyed the dimensions of the room. "I want a small carousel installed right over there."

Zach was amazed. "Aren't we a little big for a carousel?"

"Oh please, Daddy. It would be just a little bigger than the ones you see in front of supermarkets, with four horses. I want it all shiny, in bright colors." She turned to him, pleased with her decision. "Wouldn't you like to ride one?"

"No."

"But you would, if we had one."

"I would if I paid for one. Where do you get such a thing?"

"There you go! Let's look into it, please?"

"I don't understand."

"The whole room is going to be done in a carnival motif. Don't you get it? A cotton candy machine, a popcorn machine, carnival posters, a helium tank for balloons and skeeball!"

He looked around the room, puzzled by her vision. "Where?"

"We'll have room."

"We have *a* room. I don't know if all these…interesting things you want will fit in it."

"Trust me."

"That's all I can do." He put an arm around her as they continued walking through the silent, empty house. "We need to talk about something, baby."

"Something bad?" She looked concerned.

"I don't think of it that way."

"That's good."

"Do you still want to meet Marquel?"

"Hell yeah!"

"I beg your pardon?"

"I mean, yes."

"Okay, I'm going to be honest with you, Jackie. So don't jump to any conclusions…but, I've been seeing Marquel outside of the office."

"You mean dating her?"

He nodded.

"*Cool!*"

"I'm glad to hear you feel that way. Maybe what I'm trying to tell you won't bother you."

"What?"

"I've asked her to live with me. In this house." He watched as her face clouded over. He could see tears forming in her eyes.

"Daddy," she choked, "but this is our house. Yours and mine. You said we could ask mother about changing the arrangement."

"That hasn't changed." He reached out to stroke her hair, but she jerked away.

"I thought it was going to be *our* house." She turned away from him, wiping her tears.

"It is ours, but honey, I care very much for Marquel. I know you're going to like her too."

"I don't want to meet her."

"You just said…"

"I don't care what I said. Now I'm being forced to *like* her."

"No one's forcing you to do anything, Jackie."

She swallowed hard, looking at him hopefully. "Do you love her?"

He was afraid of where all this was going. "Yes."

"Oh God!" she cried, then quickly turned and ran until she was out the front door.

He caught up with her by the car and tried to reassure her that his love for Marquel in no way detracted from his love for her.

"But why now?" She held to him tightly. "Couldn't we just live here a little while, alone?"

She was pleading with him, begging. Her sobs were broken by sudden gasps as she let her emotion overcome her.

"Baby, calm down." He held her. He had no idea it would come to this, and he knew there was no way he could ask Marquel to wait. The only way he could see to resolve this was to get Jackie and Marquel together before anyone moved in.

It broke his heart to know Jackie had been counting on this moment and he'd shattered it for her. He'd been totally insensitive to the importance she had placed on the house.

"Make a deal?" He tilted her chin up.

"What?" She brushed the back of her hand over her nose.

"I've been unfair, I admit it. But I can't turn my back on either one of you…Marquel has…problems, honey."

Jackie didn't seem convinced, but she listened anyway.

"You two have to meet eventually, so why don't we all get together? Before anyone moves in."

"But…"

"But nothing, Jackie. You can extend yourself that much."

She started to cry again. "You make it sound like the house was all your idea, like you're ready to dump me if I give you a hard time."

"Don't be ridiculous."

"I don't want to meet Marquel. And I hope she decides she doesn't want to live with you either!"

Zach didn't bother to say another word. He recognized the stand-off. It was one of the many defense mechanisms in Jackie's arsenal. He would have to deal with the situation. For now, he'd let her believe she'd had the last word.

The crowded shopping mall was packed with soap groupies craning their necks to get a look at this season's contenders. Joyce Oswald was representing the nighttime soap category, while various daytime stars were parading down the small L-shaped runway, waving and strutting to various soap themes played over the mall intercom. The crowd screamed, drowning out most of the music. The mall manager busied himself passing out cordless mikes to the five stars as they sat and began taking questions.

Collins stood against a pillar next to the entrance of Lily Rubin. Joyce, he observed, had dressed especially demure, as if anything about the woman could be called demure. Her full maxi length skirt and long-sleeved silk blouse in turquoise and black were tame, compared with her usual, near bare-breasted party attire.

"Can you keep a secret?" she asked in a stage whisper. The crowd roared. "I was talking to Ty Mayo recently, creator of *Suburban Life*, and he's thinking about a spin-off for Melissa."

Hands flew in the air.

Collins was amused by her grandeur. So far, she had controlled the mall event, leaving her fellow actors holding what might as well be dead mikes.

She answered all of five questions and said, "My throat is about to give out. Let me get some water and you all can ask the other guys some questions."

She departed the stage and Collins moved in quickly toward the platform exit. He knew she had no intention of getting back up there. She only wanted to get things stirred up enough to make the other stars appear boring.

"Joyce." He waved.

She turned, her eyes narrowing to slits. "*You!*"

"Who else? I can tell you're pleased to see me."

"Did ya get my news up there? Go ahead and print it. I expect one page."

"How is it you can speak English for the audience, but assault the rest of us with garbled slang?"

"This is me, baby. That hoity-toity shit is for them. They pay the bills."

"Mayo really working something up for you, or are you just trying your hand at free publicity?"

"You're the investigative journalist, go figure it out."

"I'll do that."

"Gonna call Ty, huh?"

"Start at the source."

She laughed. "He's considering the series, believe me."

"I believe you. Got anything new on your co-star?"

"Please, she's sleeping with her shrink. It's all very boring."

"Zach Manning?"

"That's the one."

"She have any more psychotic episodes?"

"Get lost, blondie. Make something up and leave me alone. Unless you wanna interview me for your rag." She paused, he shook his head. "What's so fuckin' special about that bimbo?"

"Come here." He grabbed her arm.

She twisted free. "I don't want ya grabbing me, ya hear? I'm tellin' ya to bug off. If I ain't worth a headline, you ain't worth my time."

The mall manager approached them. "Are you okay, Ms. Oswald?"

She cleared her throat. "This man is upsetting me. He tried to grab me."

Collins hands went up. "I'm leaving, dough boy."

"Good riddance!" Joyce spat.

CHAPTER TWENTY-FOUR

Sophie was more delighted than Isabel could imagine. Not only was her oldest and dearest friend complaining about her handsome and distinguished ex-husband, but she was also complaining about the number one media star in recent months. Until today, Sophie had only heard rumors of Zach Manning's liaison with the starlet. Now it was confirmed, and Sophie was going to get an earful.

"I swear to God, Sophie, if that man thinks he can shack up with a bimbo and expose his daughter to that kind of behavior… he's got another thing coming." Isabel was positively seething.

"Oh dear, tell me, how is Jackie taking all this?" Sophie tried the concerned approach and made a sad face at the receiver. Then smiled. She was getting into this!

"She's sulking, not eating…she's just heartbroken. Lyle and I tried to cheer her up by taking her to Disneyland, but she just moped around." Isabel wanted to scream but thought the effort would be wasted. "Honestly, Lyle even offered to buy her this huge Winnie the Pooh for her collection and she refused him outright."

"How awful." Sophie covered the mouthpiece. She was almost snickering. Surely this was the first time Isabel and Lyle had bothered to do anything with the poor girl. She could almost picture Isabel riding Dumbo, trying to keep her hair in place. Jackie must have felt like Cinderella, being escorted to the ball with an ogre on either side. Only instead of meeting the prince, she got to watch him dance with everyone and then leave.

"Sophie, dear, be honest with me. You've had that woman at your parties. Is she psychotic?"

"Not that I could tell. But her agent did urinate in one of my closets."

"How ghastly!"

"Actually, it was quite amusing. From the account I got, he had walked into the bedroom with Spike McKenzie of Tone Deaf and Joi Hickaby, you know, that cute girl who married Rudy Barroll, Courtney's ex? Anyway, they were really going at it when Avery walked in. He was holding himself and dancing around. Joi pointed to a set of doors and Avery picked door number one. Wrong. So the end result was he pissed all over my Vuitton luggage."

"How can you laugh about that?"

"What should I do? After all, he happens to represent the hottest…sorry."

Isabel sighed. She knew Sophie was right. Marquel may be screwing her ex-husband, but the woman was a hot property. "Soph, I have to pick up Jackie at aerobics now. Thanks for lending an ear."

"Don't mention it. Are you up to lunch tomorrow?"

"I can't, dear. Lyle and I are meeting some of his associates for lunch. Maybe towards week's end?"

"Don't hesitate to call. Give Jackie my love."

"I will." Isabel slammed the phone into its cradle.

What the hell was she going to do?

CHAPTER TWENTY-FIVE

Zach somehow managed to convince Jackie he would devote as much time, if not more, to being with her. This allowed him to make the move with Marquel a little less stressful. He was beginning to think *he* needed some professional help.

The move had been a semi-chaotic experience. First, he had Jackie order for the great room and her room, organizing on Fridays and Saturdays, and Marquel arranging for the rest of the house Sunday through Thursday. He managed to keep each from seeing the other until the time that was agreed upon. Marquel and Jackie were to have dinner together in a few weeks. In the meantime, each got to inspect the other's decorating techniques.

Jackie's taste was bold and bright, utilizing primary colors and hi-gloss finishes, while Marquel settled on soft tones of powder blue, peach and gray. Zach let the women each do as the pleased, and, to his surprise, neither of them complained about the other's taste in color, scheme or furnishings.

Marquel, having given up her place, insisted Lawanda be their housekeeper. Zach agreed without hesitation, asking only that the woman live outside the home. Anticipating Jackie's eventual move, he didn't need three women ganging up on him.

"Zach, you know what I love most about this place?" Marquel squeezed his hand.

"What?" He'd fallen asleep in a lounge chair by the pool. He had not realized that she'd been trying to get his attention.

"The privacy. I love us being here without anyone to bother us, even without Lawanda trying to bring us lunch." She rubbed her hand on his chest. "I like doing these things myself."

"Would you lay off Lawanda and clean the place too?" He propped himself up on his elbow, the hazy sun bronzing his Mediterranean smile.

"No thanks! Anyway, Lawanda's like a sister, and I want to help her in every way I can. Besides, who said *you* wouldn't be cleaning?"

"I get dishpan hands and you know a foot massaged from a dishpan hand isn't as pleasant as the supple feel of these babies." He fanned his hands out.

"Well," she laughed, "since you put it that way…"

"You know what I love about this place?"

"What?"

"Skinny dipping at midnight."

"We haven't done that."

"We will tonight."

"Is that a date?"

"It's a promise." He sat up. "I'll grill some shrimp, you can make a salad…I'll bring the wine."

"Sounds good."

"Dress code is a terry robe, with a splash of your best perfume."

"Sounding even better." Marquel sighed. "Too bad I'm busy tonight."

"Doing what?"

"I'm supposed to see my psychiatrist…he's very ticklish about cancellations."

"Tell him you're seeing your sex surrogate tonight."

"Just seeing him?"

"In session with him."

From the other side of the wall, Collins watched the actress roll over and remove her bathing suit top. The good doctor doused her with tonic water and before long the two were wrestling in the pool.

Dave had the shot of them tumbling into the pool. Collins hoped like hell he caught the actress's reflection in the sliding glass door so it would show she was topless.

"Did you know they were going to skinny dip?" Dave asked.

"We're voyeurs, not perverts." Collins clamped his jaw. "Get some more shots before we go, I wanna get these pictures in tonight for next week's edition."

"Maybe I'll come back." Dave grinned, snapping away while the motor drive droned. "Around midnight."

"I won't have you blowing this. There's too much mileage I can get out of this broad. The last thing we need is you falling out of one of their trees or getting eaten by the neighbor's Rottweiler."

Dave sneered. "Your mileage…I could sell those prints for some big money. Yes. A little humping by the pool could make the next few months very comfortable for me. I'm in, whether you like it or not."

"Then you're on your own. If you're in, you're out as far as I'm concerned."

"You're breaking my heart." Dave grabbed a cigarette from Collins' pack and lit it.

"We have a gala in Barbados next week. That's the agenda."

The photographer twisted the cigarette between his thumb and index finger. "I might have to think about this."

Collins peered back at the couple in the pool. They were totally unaware. He almost pitied them.

Dave flipped his cigarette across the yard. "If you can get me double for these," he held up a can of film, "I'll back off."

"Done." Collins grinned at his victory. "Don't worry, Dave, we're far from finished here."

Ken fidgeted with a pen holder. Almost every phone line was blinking, but he swore to himself that Terry would have to learn to handle the calls without his help.

"Ken," she panted over the intercom, "I have Marquel on line two and Mr. Peters on line four."

"Take it easy. You sound like you're hyperventilating. I'll take four, you tell Marquel to hold, or get her number and I'll call her back."

"Okay."

Ken punched the flashing button with a pencil eraser. "Jon, great to hear from you...the deal...whoa! You know it...lunch? Let me see here, Friday's open...sure...Friday it is." He hung up. "Holy Guacamole!" He screamed. "Jon Peters. Jon *Batman* Peters...calling *me*! Oh shit, Friday. What will I wear?"

He got up, dancing about the room. "Wait a minute, he didn't tell me what he wanted...ah, who gives a shit? I'm in...I'm..."

Terry walked in.

"What?"

"Marquel's on line two, waiting. Is everything ok?"

He grabbed Terry by the shoulders, hugging her, then pushing her back. "Does the name Bat-fucking-man mean anything to you? Get out there and do something secretarial...and expect a bonus this week!"

Ken watched the doe-eyed girl back out of his office and shut the door.

"The bimbo's getting a raise...She managed to not disconnect Jon Peters! That's my girl..." he blew a kiss at the door.

He slid back into his chair and propped his feet up on the desk. "Hello, beautiful."

"Ken?"

"Honey, I am on cloud nine over here..."

"That's good." Marquel wondered if he'd been drinking.

"I'm glad you called. I've got a script for you that came in a few days ago...a new production company...Far East. Three guys from New York who decided to make films in L.A. You're going up against some heavies, so read it tonight. Terry's cousin will deliver it."

"Her cousin?"

"I need a messenger and the kid actually has more brains than Terry does. Which isn't hard to believe when you think about it. His name is Harry, but don't let him in the house."

"I might be out, but he can leave it with Zach."

"How are the two of you, anyway?"

"He's the most loving man I've ever met, Ken. And the reason I called...I wanted to ask you about the interview with *Preview* magazine...they want to come to the house. I'd rather not. After all, it's Zach's place. I'd like to keep things here private."

"You don't know how happy that makes me." *You really don't.* "I'll see what we can do."

"Thanks."

"I'll send that script as soon as I can. I need it back before someone else moves on it."

"Okay, tonight."

"Call me tomorrow?"

Zach took a pull of the martini and looked at his daughter. "It's just as hard for her as it is for you, baby."

"What, talking?"

"Opening up."

"What's her problem, anyway? Is she completely mental?"

"I'll thank you to keep remarks like that to yourself." He gritted his teeth. "I could send you home in a taxi...but get this straight, you are not now or ever privy to any information concerning patients. And if you keep this up, I'll make you sorry you came. Is that clear?"

Jackie pouted. At least Marquel wasn't going to end up drunk like her father. Martinis weren't a good sign. "Then what do we talk about?"

"You two can figure that out all by yourselves."

Marquel walked back into the bar. Her Santa Fe chambray skirt and silver-studded blouse had caught the eye of many a patron. Whispers were beginning to elevate.

Zach stood, letting her take his seat next to Jackie. "Excuse me."

"Daddy..." Jackie's eyes followed him as he walked out of the dimly lit room.

"You think we should eat here in the bar?" Marquel asked her, taking a deep breath before she went on. "Or wait for a table in the dining room?"

"Huh?"

"We can do that, you know, eat at the bar."

"Right here?" Jackie pointed to the countertop.

"Yes. The dining room looked kind of stuffy. In here we have a better excuse for poor table manners."

"I don't mind," she shrugged, "if Daddy doesn't."

"Let's ask him."

"I didn't think adults liked having…kids around in the bar."

"Look, we're both having a difficult time with this. I just thought we'd get a better chance to acquaint ourselves in a casual atmosphere." Her smile confused the girl. Marquel's hopes diminished as the girl's expression turned to disgust.

"Daddy," she addressed her father when he returned, "do you want to eat here in the bar?"

"Sure. If you ladies would like to, that is."

"I guess that's that." Jackie tried to smile.

Once they had some steaks and onion rings with lots of ketchup, the threesome developed into a more talkative group. Marquel had shared stories of outtakes on the set that had them all laughing.

On the ride home, everyone was busy singing along to Paul Simon's *Graceland*. Dinner was the pre-test, but now the three of them would spend their first night together in the house.

Zach went to bed early, purposely, to allow the two some time to get to know one another. They stayed up until well past two in the morning, eating cotton candy and riding the miniature carousel that Zach had purchased from a collector.

It seemed everything would be fine.

Then Marquel departed to Zach's room.

Jackie felt confined to her part-time bedroom. She almost longed for the days at Century City when she would meet her father's famous neighbors and delight in their attention. Instead, he had sold the condo and she felt closed up behind the walls of Marquel's fortress. A fortress that would be a retreat for her father and Marquel. A fortress she would be allowed to visit only when it was convenient.

CHAPTER TWENTY-SIX

George sat in his truck outside the new Winn Dixie super-market in Chiefland waiting for the doors to open. Though he usually picked up milk and eggs at Bob's General Store, he decided to go all out and buy groceries for the month.

Stretching, he yawned, then took another sip of the coffee that Tiffany had personally carried out to him as he finished cleaning his tools. He had stopped eating breakfast at the diner weeks earlier to avoid the bubbly blonde. Instead, he went to the McDonald's drive-thru or ate at home.

So now she brought him hot coffee in a Styrofoam cup every morning that she had paid for herself, and she wouldn't accept his money or a tip. She called it a present, saying she hoped he'd see fit to eat at her place sometime. Have a little home-cooking.

The idea made him sick. He didn't want to be pressured by anyone, and her persistence and daily appearances were annoy-ing. When the electronic doors opened, George got out of his truck, tossing the empty coffee cup to the floor of the cab.

Inside the supermarket, he grabbed a shopping cart and pushed it along as he stopped first at the produce, then the dairy aisle. There were only a handful of shoppers in the store and he felt relieved by the quiet.

His eyes were getting heavy as they did almost every morning around this time. He wanted to get home in time to fish a little before he went to sleep. It was nice having a small stretch of creek behind the cabin.

With a stockpile of groceries filling his cart, he made for the checkout stand. There he unloaded everything, withdrawing his checkbook from his back pocket. It was odd. He could feel the hair on the back of his neck stand straight up, giving him a feverish sensation. He glanced around, certain someone was watching him. Then he saw her.

The blonde, almost white hair was unfamiliar, but her eyes pierced through him. The lavender-blue gems gleamed. They were glassy, almost like marbles. Something caught in his throat. He felt certain he was choking as he clutched the counter to keep his balance.

The cashier was busy pushing his groceries over the scanner when she noticed him turning a sickly white. "Mister...you all right?"

He reached for the tabloid, but no sooner had he touched its rough colored texture than his eyes darted to the headline. Her name. A guttural, almost animal noise escaped him. He hadn't even read the headline, he only had to see the name. Marquel.

"Oh God..."

He glanced desperately at the clerk and the bag boy. He couldn't speak. His heart pounded against his ribcage, causing him to feel as though he would buckle.

No one said a word. They wondered if the man was having a heart attack. His expression of utter horror made them unsure if he was off balance or maybe even had a pistol under his jacket.

George tried breathing slowly, inhaling and exhaling several times, hanging onto the counter with shaking hands. He didn't know what to do. His eyes watered as he looked again at the picture and the name. He had to get out of there.

He pushed past the bag boy and ran out the door, dropping to his knees beside his truck. He threw up. His insides were erupting. He heaved several times, but nothing more came up. Wiping his mouth with his jacket sleeve, he forced himself up on wobbly legs and climbed into the truck. He noticed a few people in the parking lot staring at him. The cashier had followed him out.

"You need a doctor?" She called to him. "We can call..."

He started the ignition, his eyes still burning from the nausea and pain he was feeling. Without a thought, he gunned the Bronco's engine and sped away from the shopping center.

CHAPTER TWENTY-SEVEN

Marquel put the small headphones over her ears and turned the dial up. The easy listening music was just mellow enough to lull her to sleep. She glanced over at Zach who was busy reading the *Wall Street Journal*. His reading glasses perched halfway down the strong line of his nose. He looked very distinguished. She still couldn't believe they were taking this trip. He had originally wanted to visit Aspen, but instead decided on Estes Park. She had never been to Colorado.

Zach assured her Estes Park was a quaint tourist town with cabins, hotels and small shops, not quite as congested as Aspen or Vail this time of year. "Are you sleepy?" Zach pulled off his glasses, giving her hand a gentle pat.

She nodded.

"Rest up then, because we're going to have some fun when we arrive."

"I already am." And she meant it. She hadn't had a vacation since she'd moved to California.

Zach returned to his reading and she turned to the window watching the billowy vapors of clouds. Could it be possible she'd found the love of her life? Zach was everything she could ever want in a man and more. She'd never known an individual more patient or loving, always putting those he cared for ahead of himself. She was especially proud of his relationship with his daughter. He was a wonderful father. She wondered if she would have the same compassion and understanding with children that he had.

She enjoyed Jackie, though there were difficult moments. Children like the Clip twins gave her strong feelings of inadequacy. She could never quite grasp what the emotion was, just that the more time she spent with them, the greater the depression and darkness that encompassed her. It was hard, loving Zach and yet knowing she would never want to bear him a child. She knew she would be incapable of caring for a child. Also, she feared that whatever plagued her mental health could be passed onto offspring, making the decision all the more clear.

She felt tears wash over her eyes and a lump rise in her throat. It was so damned hard trying to have a good time when she realized these things about herself. Who would waste a lifetime loving an emotional time-bomb? She herself didn't know when the moods would overcome her. Sometimes she felt she'd be better off hospitalized.

Zach pulled off his reading glasses. He sensed her mood, handing her his handkerchief.

"I'm happy," she said. "Really, I am. That's why I'm crying." She laughed.

"I'm happy too." He squeezed her hand.

"A penny for your thoughts."

"You wouldn't believe me," he said.

"Try me."

"Well, I was just thinking…we're going to look like a couple of old marrieds wearing our matching sweaters."

She laughed, dabbing at her nose with the handkerchief. They had purchased several sweaters and other heavy clothing at I. Magnin for the trip.

"I think that's sweet."

"That's exactly what I was thinking."

She glanced out the window.

The thought of growing old with this man was inviting. But was it realistic?

Jackie plopped down beside her snoring mother, pulling Isabel's right arm. The huge king-sized bed was stiff and unyielding, the way Isabel liked it.

Her mother always looked so unattractive in the morning. *No wonder Daddy divorced her.* Jackie almost giggled. The woman snored like a lioness, her mouth forever open, gasping for air. The sleep mask concealed her to some extent. Jackie never understood how any man could awake wanting to date her again.

"Mother...Mother." She shook her.

Isabel snorted. "Wha...what?" She sat up and peeled off the mask, her hair standing out on the sides like stretched wings. "What is this about, Jackie?" She glanced at the digital clock. "It's six o'clock."

"I couldn't sleep. I've been up all night thinking about Daddy and...Marquel."

"Oh." Isabel was quiet, her bloodshot eyes assessing her daughter.

"I love Daddy. But I don't know if he really cares about me."

"With that woman around...he's blind." She fluffed her pillows and sat up, focusing on Jackie.

"I mean, I know he loves me...but I think..." She started to cry, her earlier humor diminished by the thought of her father loving...his lover more than his own daughter. "I think he loves her more."

"Honey, the woman has a problem and he feels sorry for her."

Jackie let out a loud wail and fell into her mother's arms. It had been a long time since her mother had taken an interest in her and it felt good. She tried to speak but started crying again.

"Jackie, please sit up and let's discuss this, woman to woman." She dabbed the girl's tears with her thumb. "That's better. Now tell me all about it."

"I kind of like Marquel...but I just can't stand it when she goes into his room at night. It makes me sick."

"He should be more considerate of your feelings. Have you told him how you feel?"

"No."

Isabel didn't have much room to talk. Jackie knew Lyle spent more than a few evenings in her bed, but the girl never seemed to care. Or did she? "Try talking to him about it."

"But she *lives* there. He can't tell her to stay in a guest room I'm around."

"Would it make a difference if she did?"

"I wish she didn't live there at all."

"I know...your father is so unthinking. Don't worry, honey, Mommy will fix things." She hugged Jackie tight.

Zach would regret hurting his baby, she'd see to it. And with any luck, Marquel would be packing in no time. This affair surely couldn't last.

CHAPTER TWENTY-EIGHT

George had no idea how to get ahold of Marquel. After the emotional upheaval of seeing her photo, he didn't know if he was even up to searching her out. Where the hell was he supposed to start?

He paced the front room of the cabin, running his hands through his hair. His whole body ached. It had been over twenty-four hours since he'd eaten or slept. He didn't feel like working. God knew he didn't have the energy. He hadn't cried since she left. Since...

He grabbed the newspaper and rummaged through the pages. He found the daily television schedule, but the show wasn't listed. This was the only place he could start. He ran to the bin outside where he kept his old newspapers, going through each one until he found the show.

Suburban Life. He laughed bitterly. They'd never lived such an existence. What could she know about it? Rural life maybe. They had purposely avoided the suburbs.

Now that he knew which network carried the show he could try long distance for the number. All the studios were in California, that much he knew. All he had to do was call and explain, ask for her.

Explain what? That he had to talk to her? They'd think he was crazy. But what else was he supposed to do? He went back inside and picked up the phone, dialing zero. He hung up before the operator answered. He didn't need this. Not when he was finally getting on with his life. But he had to know why, and if she was going to stay out there. He swallowed. Picking up the receiver, he started again.

This time he got the studio number. He figured if he didn't call now, he wouldn't have the energy to call later. "I'm trying to reach Mar…" He hung up.

He couldn't say it. *God help me,* he thought. *I can't say her name.* He dialed again and the studio operator answered.

"*Suburban Life*, Marquel, where can I reach her?"

"Everyone's gone home, sir. Have you tried her agent?"

"Could you give me that information?" He could barely breathe.

"The office is closed, sir, but I do know off-hand that Preferred Talent represents her. Her agent is Ken Avery."

"Thank you." He pressed the button, disconnecting the conversation and listened to the dial tone.

He believed he might be able to sleep tonight. He could get the number tomorrow. His mind needed rest. Everything—his fingertips, chest, limbs—was numb. He put his head down on the kitchen table, too overwrought to think. He would call in tomorrow. He'd leave Ted and the bastards at the garage. Let them wonder where loyal old George was.

CHAPTER TWENTY-NINE

Once they had settled into the lodge, Zach and Marquel lounged about their suite enjoying some champagne and watching the warm inviting fire crackle in the fireplace.

Zach wanted to unwind before dinner, but they ended up in bed. After the hustle of shopping and flying, it felt good to be out of the bulky winter clothing and wrapped around each other, flesh against flesh.

"What do you say we ring for room service?" Zach reached down and pinched her cheek.

"Are we going to spend the entire trip in this room?"

"It's not a bad idea."

"Don't you get cabin fever?"

"Not in a suite."

"Suite fever."

"That sounds inviting. Is it anything like a sugar rush?"

She moved in close, nipping at his ear. "Room service sounds inviting too."

"What would you like?"

"Something that will give me enough energy to keep up with you...old man."

He laughed. "What on earth would make you say such a thing?" He pulled the sheet up over their heads.

They ate surf and turf by the fire and made love again beside the hearth.

The following day they roamed the town, walking everywhere they went. They stopped at an antique photography studio and had their picture made. She dressed in a corset and bloomers with her hair in disarray, and he as a soldier, his jacket unbuttoned, exposing his chest. They ate lunch at a nearby pub and stopped for a nightcap in the lodge, just before retiring to their room.

The next day they tried skiing, but neither managed well. Instead, they opted to build a snowman—trading their skis for a snowmobile. They traveled down some trails, settling on a spot to build their snow couple. The Frigids, they called them.

It seemed the time passed too quickly. Days earlier they were unpacking and now it was time to tell this winter wonderland goodbye. It didn't seem fair.

Angel voice, "George on line one."

George? "George who?"

"He asked for you, said his name is George. I thought you knew him."

Christ. "Avery here." Ken nibbled at some caramel popcorn.

"I'm trying to locate…my wife."

"You're George?"

"Yes."

"Please hold." He buzzed Terry. "This George is looking for a wife. His wife. Why the hell don't you screen my calls?"

"He asked for you," she panted.

You're pissing me off. He punched the flashing button, "George, where were we?"

"I was saying that I'm trying to locate my wife. I haven't seen her in a few years." George felt stupid all of a sudden. It all sounded like something he'd made up. Why was he so damn nervous? "But I saw her picture recently. I'm trying to find…Marquel."

"Let me get this straight," Ken pushed his tongue against his front teeth, dislodging a popcorn kernel, "you're looking for Marquel…she's your wife?"

"Yes…"

Ken laughed. "Every guy in the US is after the woman and I'm supposed to hand her over to you? Nice try." He disconnected the man.

"Terry!" He didn't bother with the intercom. He was pissed, yelling at the top of his lungs.

CHAPTER THIRTY

Marquel tossed and turned, feeling as though she were suffocating. The heat from the sun was scorching, yet in the shadows all cooled to a gentle breeze. It always started this way, drifting into a difficult sleep. A hypnotic sleep.

She looked up, but her vision was shielded by the delicate figure standing before her. She couldn't make out the woman's face; the sun had blinded her. She knelt and began picking daisies, carefully placing them in her apron pockets. She handed one to the woman.

"For me?" The voice was a soothing caress.

"Yes, Mommy."

"Thank you. Come, let Mommy give you a kiss." The woman planted a soft kiss on the child's cheek. "Daisies are my favorite."

"Me too, Mommy." The child loved to please her mother.

"Shall we put these in water?"

The child smiled, and they held hands as they walked back to the small frame home. "I can save a daisy for Daddy. Is that a good idea?"

"A very good idea. He'll be very happy."

"I like flowers."

"Daddy's going to be home soon, and I need my helper to set the table." She squeezed her hand.

"I'm a good helper."

They spent the time quietly preparing supper. Her mother tossed a garden salad and baked corn muffins while she set the table, putting the daisies one by one into a glass of water.

"Where are my girls?" A male voice drifted in as the screen door slammed behind him, muffling his next words. The man and woman talked for a moment before he walked over to the table and knelt beside the child.

"How's my girl?" He mussed her hair.

"Fine."

"Honey," he called to his wife, "did you hear this? She says she's fine. What a big girl."

She couldn't make out his face either. The crackling fire in the fireplace shone around him in a brilliant orange glow. All she could see was a shadowy figure.

"Mommy..." She was running toward the kitchen, but she tripped. It startled her. The falling motion was alarming, as though she were tumbling into a black hole. There was no one to catch her.

"Mom...my!"

She bolted upright. The tears in her eyes were hot. Her heart was racing, slamming against her ribs. Zach was beside her. She hadn't screamed...she was certain. She covered her eyes, rubbing at the fresh tears. Her heart ached now, ached for the little girl in the dream.

CHAPTER THIRTY-ONE

"Would you like another drink, sir?" The stewardess leaned in, the smell of her breath mints invading his nostrils.

"Another beer, please." He tried to smile.

He was so damned nervous he didn't know how to act. He'd never been on a plane before. The experience wasn't terrifying, just different. It was like flying across the world in your living room. Watch a movie, have a drink, eat a meal.

"Here you go." She handed him the bottle as he handed her the cash.

If it hadn't been for the agent, he probably wouldn't have made the trip. After four calls and being put down and put off, Avery hadn't believed him. There was no way George could reach Marquel by phone. He didn't know who to call. Letters were just as pointless, if not more. He just needed to talk to her, get her to explain.

He wanted answers, he *deserved* them. And if she wanted, he'd stay out of her life forever. But he had to find out why she'd done this. He took a swig of beer and tried to concentrate on the movie, *Working Girl*. He couldn't seem to get interested. He closed his eyes.

No sooner had he started to doze, when Breath Mints reentered his airspace.

"Would you like a pillow?" she whispered.

"No." He whispered back. She was as annoying as Tiffany. "Please, Miss, I'm fine."

"Yes sir."

He closed his eyes again. This time the sensation of recent events closed over him. He gave in to sleep, weak and numb. It felt as if his entire being could melt and form to the airline seat.

It didn't feel like traveling—rather, he was floating through space, trying to recapture something he'd lost long ago. If only it were that easy. His head tossed from side to side, the rest of his body immobilized. It was useless. He'd been drugged by the Sandman—the joker of the subconscious, the jester of secrets.

They strolled down Rodeo Drive taking in the afternoon sun, window shopping and observing the who's who around them. Jackie had to force herself to be open minded. Secretly she was aware of her own growing acceptance of Marquel. But it was way too soon for her to admit it.

Marquel had wanted to take Jackie to lunch, but the girl declined. Marquel would win too easily then, and what would Jackie have to show for it? Besides, Isabel was going to talk to Zach about the way he'd left her out. What good would it do to come home from shopping with an armful of treasures, laughing and giving in?

"Zach? Ken Avery. Listen, have you got a minute?"

Zach looked at his watch. "About five of them before my eleven o'clock arrives. How can I help you?"

Neither of the men had much contact with one another since Marquel began seeing Zach. He wondered what Ken could want.

"It could be nothing, Zach. God, I don't know…has Marquel ever mentioned a husband?"

It was though the room spun out of focus. Zach landed hard in his chair, feeling the coffee he drank an hour ago rising in his throat.

"I'm sorry; sometimes I just blurt things out. This must shock the holy hell out of you too, but let me say this much…it's very likely this guy is just a nutcase. You know, a celebrity stalker."

"Marquel...of course, any information she gives me is confidential." Could this be? He was a fool, an idiot to get involved with her. To fall in love with her not knowing...

He had closed his mind to her finding her identity. When he *knew* better. She was a patient, and he'd treated her selfishly, thinking of himself. Wanting her to himself.

"What do you think?"

He hadn't been listening. "I'm sorry, what did you say?" Annet buzzed, announcing his eleven o'clock appointment.

"Let's not worry about this George Jennings character..." Ken rambled. "He hasn't called in a week anyway. I think he's cooled off, given up. For God's sake, he could be another Mark David Chapman."

"That's reassuring. Good thinking, Ken. Are you intending to say that to Marquel?"

"I didn't mean..."

Zach felt his forehead, expecting a sudden fever. "I know. Where did he call from? Is he local?"

"I don't know." Ken grew quiet. He hadn't asked the man a question or given the slightest impression that he cared. Rather, he ridiculed the man instead, when he could've gotten information, had him checked out. "I never asked, but my hand to God, Zach, if he calls again, I'll get all the information I can."

"Ken...I..." Zach covered his mouth. He could lose her, just as easily as this man could jog her memory. She was entitled to her past, entitled to know...and he hadn't been helping her. "We're not saying a word about this to Marquel. We don't know a thing about the man..." he broke off.

"Mum's the word. Listen, I'll call the minute I learn anything. You'll be the first to know."

"Thanks." He hung up the phone and laid his head on the desk. His temples pounded as he clenched his teeth, grinding them at the anger that was swelling inside him. He didn't know whether to mourn or rage. How could he tell her? He couldn't... but it might trigger something.

He didn't know how to handle this. She wasn't his patient anymore, she was his lover. His life. He slammed a fist on the desk. Annet buzzed again. He didn't give a damn. Let them wait. What the hell good was he to anyone?

He couldn't even help the woman he loved. Who else was floundering through life hopelessly, thanks to good ol' Zach? Zach the quack. He laughed bitterly. What the fuck!

Annet sent the patient in after a moment. He took his seat, deciding that this may very well be his last appointment, the end of his practice.

CHAPTER THIRTY-TWO

George rather liked air travel, once they landed. Breath Mints even helped him find the rental car agency and gave him directions to the television studio.

He decided to settle into a Howard Johnson's motel for the night and check out the studio the following day. He just hoped he'd know what to say to her once he saw her.

It felt good to be away. Florida and California had similar climates, but the dazzle of Hollywood made him feel like a kid again. If only the Duke, Cooper and the rest of his favorites were still alive. He knew very little about the movies being made today. He seldom rented any, only when the weather was miserable, keeping him from fishing or hunting.

Ted...he laughed. The dumb bastard had the nerve to ask where he was going in such a hurry. The man was like a nagging wife. George wondered why Ted had never recognized his wife on television. He'd met her in passing a few times. Hell, he probably only watched *HeeHaw* or the Nashville Network anyway. Some of the guys he worked with didn't even know who was president. Why should he expect Ted to know anything about Hollywood?

He dressed in his best jeans and a powder blue pullover with a rugby collar. He had bought new clothes from the Sears catalogue more than a year ago, wearing them only a few times to the nursing home on Sundays.

The drive to the studio was hectic. He could hardly keep up with the traffic and watch for his exit at the same time. When he arrived at the studio, he knew he couldn't ask for her. He would have to take the tour, then slip off to find her. He couldn't figure out why no one believed him. Certainly Hollywood was protective, but the stars had lives outside of acting. They had a past as well as a present.

The set of *Suburban Life* was to be viewed from a soundproof room. George felt apprehensive about his chances of slipping off from the group. What would he do then? When they reached the windowed enclosure, he glanced out at the actors moving about in the brightly lit mock-kitchen. He didn't see her.

An ache swelled deep in his stomach, as though he had imagined all of it. Then he saw the platinum-cotton hair, the delicate curves that were even slimmer than he remembered. She gestured to the couple seated at the breakfast table, then looked away, her eyes directed up. At him, he was certain.

The guide suggested they move on to the next set on the tour, but George, a pale figure now, asked that he be allowed to catch his breath before joining them.

He didn't move, just stared down at her, at her expressionless face. There was no way she could see him from that distance, with the studio light reflecting off the glass…it was probably a two-way mirror anyway.

He had to get down there. He had to know. He swallowed hard, pushing himself in the direction of the tour group, but slipping through a door marked "No Admittance." The small office led to the set, where in the distance he could see they were still at work. He froze and stood, silently waiting.

When they broke for lunch, he moved into the area where he'd last seen her. Then lost her somewhere in a sea of people. He couldn't find her. Without warning, she was walking toward him.

He was startled as he fought for something to say.

She looked right at him, the violet gaze nearly sent him crashing to the floor. But she continued past him, acknowledging a blonde man who had fallen into step beside her.

She hadn't recognized him.

He couldn't believe it. She looked right through him and now she was walking away…

CHAPTER THIRTY-THREE

Zach felt like an absolute heel when he got home. There was no other word for it. Ken's call had put a damper on everything. He heard talking in the kitchen and spied Marquel and Lawanda, giggling and sipping wine coolers. They looked like a couple of high school kids sneaking a drink. They stopped talking when they saw him, then both burst out laughing.

He didn't know what to make of it, until he realized they were smashed. He was glad, because he too could then drown in a few martinis and not suffer the guilt. Or so he hoped.

The night went on like that, drinking, laughter and fun. Lawanda stayed for dinner, joining them in the great room afterward for a game of Skee-Ball. Marquel dragged Zach upstairs after bidding Lawanda goodbye and sending her home in a cab.

The wine made her giddy and she tore at his shirt, struggling so hard that the buttons flew off.

He'd never seen her this wild, never known lovemaking so powerful. It was beyond anything he'd experienced. He feared he wouldn't be able to keep up with her feverish pace, but with every touch of her hand or her mouth, he found an excitement that kept him aroused, fueling his passion.

When they had both collapsed in abandon, he found, even after she'd finally given in to sleep, he was still wide awake.

He felt like he was cracking up. The release of tension was like a silent admission of guilt, giving him a sinking sensation. But he had to think, there was no justification for telling her of today's call. If the man were a nutcase, as Ken said, he would hurt Marquel, pushing her without reason.

Remembering her heated whispers, the things she said as they made love—that she was more in love with him than she could have hoped to be, that no one had ever made her feel the way he could...

This time the guilt filtered through. What if George Jennings *was* her husband? How was he surviving without her, wondering what happened to her? Did he have any idea why she'd left?

But maybe the man was abusive, causing her to block the ugly memories of their marriage, the hurt. God knew obsessive men hunted down their ex-wives and murdered them for leaving...

He put his arm around her, drawing himself in close against her. He had no idea if a husband did exist, or a parent, a friend, a link to her past. He knew only that he loved her. Whoever she may be.

She rolled over then, opening sleepy eyes and looking at him. "Why aren't you sleeping?"

"I'm not finished loving you."

She propped herself up on her elbow. "Oh?"

He stared at her, eyes like obsidian at a burning temperature. "I love you." He had meant to tell her a hundred times before he let her fall asleep.

"And I love you."

He smiled.

"There's something I've been meaning to tell you..."

"What is it?" He could almost forget his guilt, if they could just keep loving each other like this.

"I've had this recurring dream, I think it's a memory..." she said.

He held his breath. So much for hoping to forget, even if only for the night.

"...I don't know, maybe dreams are just part of our imagination, but I think it's from my childhood. My mother and father…I couldn't see their faces, but I remembered something… after I woke up." She paused, looking at him as if for approval. "My mother's name is Joanne."

"Joanne?"

"It just came to me…but I'm certain of it."

He wondered when it was all going to open up for her, and if it would flower or snowball into a looming threat. She would be remembering more, unless something set her back. He offered a silent prayer that whatever came next, he would be capable of helping her through it.

After a night's rest, George concluded that he had to catch her alone, away from the studio. How else would he have a chance to talk to her? He couldn't stop thinking about the way she looked at him, the blank, unacknowledged glance of someone passing a stranger. It disturbed him, but it scared him more to think that maybe she—just didn't *care*. Was that logical?

But wasn't it illogical that she could have done this all to begin with? She was always shy, not likely to turn away from a familiar face. At least that was how he remembered her. Was it possible she could convince herself he didn't exist? And why would she do such a thing?

It had taken some ingenuity, but he managed to hit the studio at the end of the day, catching a glimpse of her heading for a Saab. As she sped out of the parking lot he had trouble keeping up with her.

She never drove like this, and yet, whoever she was now, did. He kept a safe distance in the Ford Escort coupe he'd rented. It was obvious she had no idea she was being tailed, and he felt satisfied that he would get the opportunity to talk to her. But he had to be careful, not jump the gun. She probably had heavy security at her place, another obstacle to overcome.

As they neared Beverly Hills, George was momentarily distracted. He stared in awe at the homes, their grounds, breathing in the stench of money in the air. It was like a fantasy, though not one of his. And not a half mile ahead of him was a woman he had known since they were both teenagers. A girl he'd loved and cared for. Protected. A woman who was now a complete stranger.

She swung left into a gap in an expanse of the iron gate. It shut automatically behind her. He could hear the electronic whine of the gate clamping…sealing her off.

He pulled up just close enough to watch her exit the car and bound into her home, a home modest in comparison to most of the palaces they'd passed.

"This is it," he said to himself.

This was the place. He would camp out, or at least check back and try to catch her on her way out. He didn't want to scare her, but he didn't want anyone else to be involved. It could get messy, someone misunderstanding his intentions. If only she weren't a celebrity, it would be so damned easy. He laughed, his bitterness filling the car's interior. It was ironic that all their good times, even the tragic, would lead to her celebrity.

Marquel.

The name made him want to scream. Why in hell did she have to take that name? It was almost blasphemy to think about. But it was something he couldn't think about. It hurt too much.

Zach greeted Marquel with a martini, but she shook her head no.

She already had a headache. Collins' little episode at the studio today hadn't helped. He wanted her to answer questions about her relationship with Zach, her doctor. He alluded to their "romance." She managed to brush him off, but she knew he was trying to get at something juicy for his little rag.

She told Zach about the incident, but he didn't seem to hear her. He was distracted by his own thoughts lately. She dropped the subject.

The phone rang a constant cry for attention and when it was obvious Zach wasn't going to answer it, she grabbed the hall phone.

"Dr. Manning, please." The voice was feminine and satin with a hint of sarcasm.

"One moment." She pushed the hold button. "Zach! For you."

He looked up, seeing the receiver hanging limply in her hand. "I'll get it in the study."

He disappeared into the back of the house.

"Zach Manning."

"Zach, it's Isabel. Do you have a moment to talk…alone?"

"Izzy? Is anything wrong with Jackie?"

"Yes and no, that's why I called." She paused for effect. "It seems your daughter feels neglected with that actress living in your house. Were you aware of that?"

"No, I wasn't. They went shopping together last week and seemed to hit it off just fine."

"It's all a front, Zach. She's been crying her eyes out." Well, not since that one night, but Zach didn't need to know that. "And you must promise you won't tell her I called you, she begged me not to tell you. I'm just worried about the effect this might have on her in the long run."

"What are you driving at?" He gritted his teeth. He knew Isabel well enough to know there had to be something in it for her when she started making threats. In all the time they'd been divorced, she only called when she wanted Jackie out of her hair, or when the girl was being rebellious.

"I'm not driving at anything. Can't you be a little concerned? You must be feeling some guilt to snap like this." She kept her cool. She knew enough about his pressure points that she could keep him guessing.

"What would I have to feel guilty about, Isabel?"

"Please, you know as well as I do that Jackie was ecstatic about your buying a house. I don't know what possessed you to move, but, she was looking forward to spending *more* time with you."

"She still can."

"With that woman always around? She feels threatened. When can she be alone with you?"

"Whenever she wants to, all she has to do is say the word."

"I don't believe that. She told me you took Marquel to Colorado…when is your daughter going to travel with you?"

He *was* feeling guilty. Isabel had a valid point, though he hated to admit it. He was still certain there was more behind her concern than Jackie's well-being. A hidden motive. He sighed. "What has Jackie been saying?"

"Not a word to her?"

"Not a word."

Isabel felt triumphant at last. "She's put off by Marquel. She feels replaced…and I don't mind saying she was more than a little upset recently. I thought she was going to have a nervous breakdown."

"I'll talk to her."

"How? You can't mention this, Zach. She would feel I betrayed her."

"You haven't, and I'm her father. I can initiate a discussion of her feelings toward Marquel."

"Well, I've already taken care of her need to get away…clear her head…"

"What are you talking about? What need to get away?" He didn't need this. Not now.

"I'm sending her abroad…Paris, to be exact. Some of her girlfriends are going to a modeling…"

"Stop right there! I won't let this happen, Isabel. My daughter is not going to Paris alone with a couple of girlfriends for any reason. What the hell made you think this up? Are you and Lyle planning an extended vacation for yourselves?"

She ignored the accusation. "I don't know what you're so upset about, Zachary. The girls will be with friends of the Barroll's. What's wrong with it? She'll only spend half of the school year there, then she's home for summer vacation. If she likes it, she can go again the following year. Wouldn't that just suit you… and Marquel?"

"Who does it really suit, Isabel?"

"Certainly not me. I'm quite happy having Jackie at home. But I don't want to stifle her growth, keep her from doing things."

"This isn't about Jackie. It's about you getting even."

"Getting even? What on earth do you mean?" She laughed.

"Let's just say you have my attention now, and you can put the idea of Jackie going anywhere out of your head."

"No."

"Don't put her in the middle; it will only upset her more... than my current relationship."

He wondered if Marquel had retired to bed, was waiting for him. He wished Jackie could get on the phone, but there was a score to settle with her mother.

"It's like this, Zach. Talk to her. I've given the go ahead. If she listens to you, she stays. Otherwise she goes."

"Fine. Tell her I'll pick her up Friday afternoon."

"Fine."

"And Isabel? Don't go making any flight reservations. My daughter is not going to any foreign country alone." He slammed the receiver into the cradle.

CHAPTER THIRTY-FOUR

George woke to the sound of a car passing at a high rate of speed.

"Shit." He jerked, then glanced in the rearview mirror. "Goddamn it!" He hit the steering wheel. He had fallen asleep sometime earlier that morning and now he had missed his opportunity. He looked at the house and noticed a man in a robe and slippers going inside. Who the hell was he? George laid on the horn. The man stared out from the doorway. George stepped out of the rental car.

"Hey, hey! I've gotta talk to you." He ran, his hands shoved deep in his jeans pockets.

"What do you want?"

"To talk. I need to get some directions, I'm lost." George stood inches from the iron rails.

Zach walked closer. "Where is it you're going?"

George didn't speak until the man got closer. "You live here?"

"Do you see many people wandering Beverly Hills in their bathrobes?"

George laughed. "Guess not. It's nice to meet someone with a sense of humor. People out here don't have much time to say hello, much less laugh."

"I suppose everyone's busy." He noticed the lines on the other man's face, the weariness about him. He wondered if perhaps the man was homeless, living out of his car. Then he noticed the rental tag.

"Are you an actor?" George asked.

"No. Try a doctor, but thanks for the compliment."

"No problem."

"Where is it you're going...or looking for?"

"Actually, I'm trying to..." he tried to think of something quick, but it had been so difficult looking at this man who was living in the same house with... "I lied. I'm out here scouting the homes of celebrities. I thought somebody famous lived here."

"What's your name?"

"George."

"Listen, George, I know you're lying. Why don't you get to the point, or shall I call the police?"

George didn't bother saying another word. He just turned and walked back to his car. Who the hell was this guy anyway?

"And George, don't come back," Zach shouted.

CHAPTER THIRTY-FIVE

Marquel felt the sudden sting, her face burned hotter. Joyce had just slapped her as hard as she could ever remember being hit.

"You bitch." She turned, swinging at the brunette and grabbing a fistful of her hair in her other hand. She pulled the woman to the floor. "You think you have the right to take your anger out on anyone?" she screamed, holding fast to a healthy clump of hair. She narrowly missed scratching the woman's face.

"Cut."

They both collapsed on the floor crying.

"Goddamn you, Sid!" Joyce screamed. The action was filmed, but the dialogue would be muted by narrative and dramatic music.

"You were great." He ran in between the two women. Joyce tripped him, and then pounced on him pounding on his belly.

"Fuck you, Sid. Fuck you. Fuck you, fuck you!" She slapped his face.

"Someone stop her." Sid called out.

"Aw, what a fucking wimp. How's it feel, Sid?" Joyce slapped him again, then stood and walked over to Marquel, offering her a hand.

They looked at one another, not saying a word. It hurt, fighting the way they did for the camera. They were supposed to fake it. How did this happen? Why were they really laying into each other?

Sid could tell, certainly, and he could also have stopped them at any time.

"Thanks." Marquel mumbled to Joyce and got to her feet, rubbing her cheek.

"Kid, if Carnie knows what's best for him, he won't ever fuck with me again."

"Joyce, I can hear you. I've had it with you," Sid came up beside her. "Start looking for work, you're outta here."

"Yeah, yeah," she laughed. "Try it."

He punched his index finger in the middle of her chest. "Kiss my ass, Joyce. You've just written yourself out of the show."

Joyce slapped his hand away and exited laughing.

Sid's threats were idle. He'd never been one to disrupt the cast. She had nothing to worry about even if he did try to fire her. She had a contract. A binding contract.

"Who could have such profound luck?" Collins said to the man at the rental car agency. "My old college roommate was driving down Santa Monica Boulevard in one of your rentals...we haven't seen each other in a couple of years. Well, I couldn't grab him. I lost the bastard on the freeway...still drives like he's in the Grand Prix. But hey, I took the rental place number and here I am."

"Can't help you," the man behind the desk mumbled. "Policy."

"You're going to keep old friends apart over policy?"

"Leave your name and number; I'll pass it on to..."

"Puke. That's what we called him."

"Puke," the man agreed distractedly.

"You know frat brothers. Anyway, here's the license number." Collins had copied the number of the car he'd seen outside Marquel's house on two occasions. He wondered if maybe there wasn't a private investigator following her, or if it was one of his competitors. A new one maybe. New guys were hungry.

"I told you..."

Collins put a fifty-dollar bill on the counter.

The man's face twisted with disgust. Then Collins put another fifty down, and another, and the disgust receded as if by magic.

"Wait here." He walked over to a desk and wrote the information on a slip of paper and returned it to Collins. "You don't know the guy, do you?"

"George." Collins laughed, reading the name. "George Puke Jennings. Of course I know him…"

"Spare me. And this conversation didn't take place, understand?"

"It's our secret." He read the paper again, noting that George had registered at a Howard Johnson's Motor Lodge. "Let's see what Puke has to say…"

The afternoon proved eventful for Collins. He pieced together more than he had bargained for. It seemed the Jennings character had traveled from Florida and had made reservations from the motel for a studio tour a few days earlier. This guy was serious… and Collins was just the man to figure out why.

He'd checked the motel several times and Jennings had yet to return. It dawned on him that Jennings might've returned to the studio. Collins jumped in his car and made his way west.

Things would be wrapping up at this hour, he knew. Funny thing, security had seen him around enough that they stopped questioning him. They knew he was a journalist and even Collins couldn't figure out why crazy Avery hadn't put a stop to his impromptu interviews. He made his way toward Marquel's dressing room. He spotted her in the hallway talking to Sam Kindred.

"Hello," he cut in.

Sam extended his right hand in a shake.

Marquel stood quietly, eyeing him suspiciously.

"Marquel." He nodded to her.

She didn't answer.

"I've run into an old friend of yours. Could we have a moment alone?"

Sam stepped back. "Later."

"I have no idea what you're talking about."

He glanced at her open dressing room door. "Could we step inside?"

"I'd rather not."

"It won't take long."

"Then explain. I'm waiting."

"Jennings. Ring a bell?"

"No."

"George Jennings. From your old stomping ground Gainesville, Florida."

"So?" Her eyes betrayed nothing, nothing whatsoever. Was there even a thought in her head?

"He's been here to see you."

"Has he? Listen, Mr. Collins, I don't have the time or the patience for you." She turned away, walking into her dressing room.

He followed. "I think you should make time. Tell me, what makes a man travel from one coast to the other for a woman, unless they were friends…or lovers? But hey, you can fill me in."

"I don't know or care who this man is or what he's doing. Get out."

"In good time." He closed the door and approached her, his hands deep in his pockets. He made no move to touch her, only to take the very air she breathed for his own. "Who is George Jennings?"

"Get the hell out! I'm warning you: if you come any closer you'll regret it."

He laughed. "Why the games?"

"I'm going to have you thrown out on your ass, once and for all." She tried to move past him, but he grabbed her arm.

"I'm tired of your secrecy shit, babe. I'm going to find out sooner or later anyway. Why don't you just tell me who George Jennings is?"

She remained calm. "Get your hands off me."

He released her.

"Since when is it protocol for reporters to manhandle celebrities?"

"Since I've been to hell and back trying to crack your story. I'm tired of the fucking mystery. I want the truth."

"You're saying *Pursuit* now honors truth in publishing?" She laughed. "If you want a story, go make one up. Dream up a little fairy tale with a nightmare ending and leave me the hell alone."

"As you wish," he bowed. "But let me warn you, you could save yourself time and embarrassment by playing along. What's your price?"

"A libel suit against *Pursuit* and its overzealous reporter."

"What's Jennings worth to you? A couple hundred G's?"

"Goodbye." She walked out, not bothering to throw him out or secure her dressing room.

Collins didn't move. He knew the price—George would open up for the almighty dollar. After all, he couldn't have much. He was staying in a HoJo.

CHAPTER THIRTY-SIX

It was a long shot, but George tried Ken Avery's number again. This time he was able to get the doctor's name and phone number from the receptionist. He couldn't believe how simple it was; he even got the phone number of their residence—the same place where he stood talking like an idiot to Dr. Zachary Manning. Now he had to call, and either to talk to Marquel or ask the doctor what he'd done to her.

He tried the house first and got an answering service, so he made a bold attempt to reach the doctor at work. Did he want to leave his name and number? No. He would call back.

By three-thirty in the afternoon he had exhausted all efforts to reach the doctor. He tried the house again at six that evening, and Zach Manning answered.

"Is this the doctor?"

"Yes, to whom am I speaking?"

"First, hear me out."

Zach sighed, but didn't speak.

"This is George Jennings. I spoke to you at the gate this morning."

"How did you get this number?"

"I wouldn't be bothering you, hell, I wouldn't even be here if someone would let me talk to her. I got your number from the agent's secretary. Too bad I didn't ask for it a long time ago." He laughed weakly. "Anyway, it's about Joanne."

"Joanne?"

"Mar…Marquel," he choked. "I call her Joanne, that's her real name."

"Who are you, George?"

"Her husband."

"Marquel's husband?"

"Yes," he said quietly.

It was all flooding back now. All the hurt, the emotion. He had so many questions to ask her, but he didn't trust this doctor.

"If you are her husband, why did it take you so long to get in touch with her, to so much as try?"

"I didn't know where she was…that she…" Why was it anyone's business what had happened between them? He wasn't the one who left her, she left him and who was this guy to care? He was probably sponging off her success. Her success—God, how did she do it?

"George…"

"She never mentioned me?"

"No." Zach grew tense. He could tell this man was a nervous wreck, whoever he was. It didn't quite fit the man he met this morning, but…

"She ever talk about anything? The past, I mean…" George stifled a sob. Jesus, how could he react this way, talking to the man who was keeping them apart?

"George, I don't understand. If Marquel was your wife…"

"She *is* my wife. Her name isn't…it's Joanne. I have a right to see her."

"Maybe she doesn't want to see you."

"Did she tell you that?"

"George, on the level, I'll tell her you called. Give me your number and if she wants to talk, she'll call you."

"How do I know you'll give her the number?"

"If she knows you, she'll call you. Trust me. I'll relay the information."

"Or you'll hear from me…I don't know what you've done to her, but you can't stop me from talking to her. You can't stop me from seeing my wife."

"What's the number?" Zach jotted the information down.

CHAPTER THIRTY-SEVEN

George hung up the phone.

He hadn't felt this drained in weeks, not since he'd seen her picture on the tabloid cover. Was he an idiot allowing this man to control the situation? Hell, he'd have to go back to Florida soon or he'd be out of cash. He rubbed his tired eyes. He couldn't go back without knowing. What sense would it make for him to have come all this way and not even get to see her or talk to her?

He fell back on the bed, massaging his temples, unable to think. The room was making him claustrophobic, closing in on him. He shut his red-rimmed eyes and began to doze. His body slowly relaxed, dissolving into the stiff mattress. He welcomed the numb sensation, the weightlessness of spirit, free of thought. He drifted into a Technicolor world of imagery and objects, timelessness and space.

In the distance someone was rapping at his door.

He tossed. It must be the dragon whose fire was extinguished when he tumbled into the marshmallow moat. Rapping at his chamber door…but the sound was out there somewhere, beyond his subconscious where the Poes' penned their madness with eloquence, and the incubus was seething…

He bolted upright, rubbing his face. He heard it again.

There was someone at the door. He went to open it, not recognizing the blonde man who stood before him.

"George Jennings?" The man extended his hand. "Mark Collins, with *Pursuit*."

George scratched his head, puzzled. "The supermarket paper?"

"Yes. May I come in?"

"What do you want?" He raised his hand, stopping the man who had already stepped over the threshold to his room.

"To talk about Marquel. That's why you're here." He pushed past George and glanced around. "I can make it worth your while. I can even help you see her, if you'll help me."

"Help you?"

"Why are you here? What's your connection, an old boyfriend?"

"You're looking for something to put in your paper. Forget it."

"Name your price."

"No price."

"Everyone has a price, George. Besides, I'll find out anyway, right? You may be the missing link, my first piece of hard evidence."

"I don't need..."

"I'm with you; I don't need any trouble either. I'm trying to make it simple. I'll even pay you for your trouble." He held both palms up.

"What are you looking for?" George pretended to sound interested.

"I could tell you were smart. How much?"

"Answer the question."

"All right. I know she came from Florida. That means you two have something in common. I know she's hiding her past for whatever reason with the dumb blonde routine. I also know she doesn't particularly want to see you."

"How do you know that?"

"She told me."

"I don't get it. She knows I'm here?"

"Yeah. She tried to act like she didn't know you...they all do that. So, what's your price?"

"What did she say about me?"

"Hey, she doesn't want to see you. Get it in your head. Hey, are you the one...?"

"The one what?"

"You know she had an abortion…"

"God, no…" George sat, his hands trembling. He was dying, he was certain of it. Would she…? Not Joanne. His stomach was sickened by the thought.

"Calm down, honey." Zach handed her a martini. "What has you so rattled?"

"Collins, he grabbed me…I had him barred from the studio, the set…I don't get it. He keeps throwing this guy's name around. It doesn't make any sense. What do I care about a fan who's trying to meet me? He's implying there's more to it…"

"Who?"

"Collins."

Zach put his arm through hers and walked her out to the patio. He was afraid he knew who Mark Collins was referring to. Ken's phone call, the man at the gate—it was all falling into place. But how much of it could be taken as fact?

He should be the one to tell her. If only George Jennings were claiming to be her brother... Or even a lover. But not her husband. "Let's relax, then take a swim."

"Perhaps." She was deep in thought. "George Jennings, that's the name he kept repeating."

Zach didn't say a word. Everything was about to snowball, and he didn't know how or whether to tell her what little he knew. All he needed was Collins and George and a barrage of media descending on her. On them. "You've never heard the name before?"

"No."

"Think…could it be a relative, a friend?"

She sipped at the martini and shook her head. "I think Collins is just trying to start something."

"Like what?"

"I don't know." She got up and paced. "Maybe he knows I've been struggling with my memory, maybe he hired someone to pose as a…I don't know…someone to make me crazy."

"Why would Collins want to make you crazy?"

"Because he doesn't like me. He's an angry young man who'll stop at nothing to get a story."

"He's got a wealth of people to follow, to expose, but to try to make you snap?"

"Goddamn it, Zach! I'm a celebrity, my life is open. Don't even try to tell me Mark Collins wouldn't stoop so low..."

Zach walked inside. He hadn't seen her this angry or upset, he didn't know what to do. But pushing this Jennings thing was not a good idea under the circumstances.

"Where are you going?" she snapped.

He stopped in the doorway. "I'm giving you some room."

"Thanks a whole fucking lot, *doc*!"

He gritted his teeth. It was a jab he hadn't expected.

She threw her glass down on the tile, shattering it into a million pieces. She laughed strangely, almost hysterically, then sat down and cried. Who did she have that really cared? No one.

Zach walked up behind her, but she hadn't heard. He gripped her quivering shoulder and she turned, falling into his embrace.

"I'm sorry," she quavered.

"Me too."

"I don't feel right about...anything. I'm scared to death of losing you."

"You'll never get rid of me." He squeezed her reassuringly, but felt just as insecure as she did. Maybe even more so. "Maybe we should talk about George Jennings."

"Let's not."

"He could be someone you once knew."

"Wouldn't he come forward if he were? Wouldn't he contact me himself?"

"You are a celebrity." He tipped her chin up. "Maybe he's tried. Maybe he can't get to you."

"And maybe he's no one."

"That's a possibility too."

She looked frightened, like a teary-eyed child. She chewed her lower lip.

"Jennings...I don't know, he might be..."

"Let's not guess."

CHAPTER THIRTY-EIGHT

Zach couldn't sleep that night for trying to decide what to do. He knew he would have to contact George himself—one way or another—before someone got to Marquel. It nagged at him for the longest time ... that he was forgetting something. Something Marquel told him about a dream.

Then it hit him. Her *mother's* name was Joanne, the same as George's alleged wife. It was too close to call...but George Jennings knew her one way or another, Zach was positive. Now it was only a matter of figuring out how, and when, to break the news to her.

CHAPTER THIRTY-NINE

Zach and Ken arranged an early meeting before Preferred opened its doors for business, before Terry arrived.

"Zach, I can't imagine what could be so urgent." Ken let Zach into his office.

"It's about Marquel, the man who called you, wanting to see her. He's called the house. Your secretary gave him the number."

"Christ," Ken muttered. "Terry is so stupid. I'm sorry, I don't know what to say."

"Don't be. I believe this man knows her. Whether or not he's her husband is another story."

"What are you saying?" Ken motioned for Zach to have a seat.

"I'm saying you've got to find the connection."

"Me?"

"Ken, you're going to lose her…We're both going to lose her if she falls apart."

They both sat, Ken looking dumbfounded, Zach appearing ill.

"What do we do?" Ken rearranged the ashtrays on his coffee table.

"First I need her file."

"File?" Ken moved the floral arrangements to the middle of the table.

"The information you have on her, references, et cetera."

"Oh." Ken grew quiet, picked up an ashtray and balanced it on his knee. "Her bio…it's all fiction," he mumbled. "We built it from the ground up, you might say."

Ken bounced his knee just as Zach grabbed the glass tray.

"You don't have anything on her at all? Not even a previous address?"

"Nope." Ken folded his arms and looked Zach in the eye. "It's done all the time. In her case it was necessary. We didn't have any information."

"Jesus Christ." Zach stood. "What now?"

"You believe this George guy is her husband?"

"Who knows?" Zach paced back and forth. "I have to talk to him."

"What'll that prove?"

"Prove...hell if I know. It might save us all some embarrassment, though. And perhaps the sanity of more than one of us... Your reporter friend is delving into the fiasco as we speak."

"Collins is no friend of mine."

"Your secretary?"

"Oh shit..." Then he shrugged. "Terry doesn't know anything, what could she tell him?"

Zach had to leave before he strangled Ken.

"Great doing business with you." He stormed out.

By four o'clock Zach had arranged his own meeting with George.

The next morning, over breakfast at a Howard Johnson's restaurant, he'd confront the mystery man. Still, nothing made sense. This George seemed calm over the phone, reasonable. It was as if he wanted to square things with Zach before moving on.

Jackie had called in tears after Zach spoke with George, wondering why he hadn't picked her up the night before. Did he love her? Was he punishing her? Should she go on to Europe as planned?

He'd forgotten all about seeing her for the weekend? His mind was racing. He had to settle things with Isabel...with Marquel... with George...God, would anything ever be normal again?

"Daddy, please, can I move in? I won't bother Marquel, I promise. I like her...she's not so bad," Jackie pleaded. She wanted her father's love, his acceptance.

She wanted to be with him.

"Baby, this is not a good time."

She cried. "It's never a good time to be with me!"

"That's nonsense. It's just that my schedule is going to be so hectic...I won't have any time..." It all sounded like excuses.

"Time! *Time!*"

"Give it a month and I promise, we'll sit down with your mother and discuss this."

"If she has anything to do with it, I won't be *here* in a month."

"Put your foot down, Jackie. She can't force you to go."

"Oh, right! Maybe she couldn't if I didn't live with her. She'll brainwash me, you wait and see."

"You're a bright girl, she can't convince you to go unless you want to."

She cried again. "Like aerobics, ballet, the docent program... those weren't my ideas."

"We'll get to your ideas in a month, I promise. Maybe sooner."

"A month." Her voice was a dead tone. "I plead for my life and it's gotta wait a month. Thanks, Daddy!" She hung up.

Zach tried to call back several times, but she'd taken the phone off the hook. How could he begin to tell her? She wouldn't understand these things and he wasn't privy to discuss them with her. He prayed she would be patient and give him enough time to get things straight.

CHAPTER FORTY

They both ordered eggs, but neither seemed to have an appetite. Instead they silently took one another apart, each wondering what she saw in the other.

"I need your help, George," Zach said.

"You need my help?" *Everyone needs my help,* he thought. Mark Collins, this guy. Didn't they know *he* needed help? That his wife must need help…

"I'll be honest with you. I'm a psychiatrist. Marquel came to me as a patient, originally. From the start she's been confused, unable to remember events from her past." He was breaking a thousand rules, and he had no idea if George could be trusted, just the gut feeling he was being sincere.

"Then you believe she's my wife?"

"I don't know what to believe."

George still couldn't bring himself to trust the doctor. It occurred to him that maybe he was being set up. "I want to talk to her alone."

"In time."

"I don't have time; I'm spending everything I've got just to be here."

"I'll loan you money if you need it."

"I don't want your money. I want to see my wife."

"Can you tell me why she came out here? Was she an actress before?"

"No. She was too shy. And she didn't look like she does now, she's changed. Do you know where she got the name Marquel?"

"No, I don't."

"She's taken someone's name...it...it sickens me...that she could do that."

Zach sat back. He didn't want to believe George, but he could see his sincerity—he was telling the truth.

The truth. Did he really want to know?

CHAPTER FORTY-ONE

Collins scaled the fence and darted to the French doors off the pool. It had been a while since he risked tripping an alarm, but this bitch was going to pay. Keeping information... hell, she was going to confide her most intimate secrets to him via his lucky bug.

It may be criminal, but he had wasted enough time fucking around, trying to be a nice guy. He was getting his story. No matter the cost, no matter the chance he was taking or the people who got hurt.

He slipped in, having gracefully sidestepped the security system. He made his way into Zach's study and rummaged through several unlocked drawers. After picking the lock on the last drawer, he found a small, semi-automatic handgun. Having found nothing of use to him, he planted the bug in a lamp on the desk. Something told him all business would be handled from this room, but just for safety's sake, he would plant another in the bedroom. God knew, from presidents to ordinary people, more was revealed through pillow talk than any other assembly.

He moved on to the great room, astonished to see the carnival décor. It seemed far removed from both the doctor's and the actress's personalities. It was too bold, too brassy. He padded up the staircase, suspecting that within the next hour someone, the gardener or maid, would make their rounds and find him. It surprised him the property was so lax in security.

He could find nothing of interest in the house, not even a kinky sex toy. The gun was it. After stopping to take a piss in their private bath, he made his way back out the way he'd come in. He was satisfied his means of investigation would produce results. Gilman had already expressed displeasure at the sluggish pace with which the story was progressing, beginning to doubt there may be a story at all.

Collins didn't care about pleasing Gilman anymore. He knew there was a story, and it was going to blow wide open. Soon. And he was going to be there.

He had gone as far as he could go now. This last step was purely for Mark Collins. Sure, he'd have a great laugh when it was all over, but it had gone far enough. She was in his blood. Nothing would stop him from exposing the root of her past. Not even getting busted for breaking and entering, invasion of privacy. Hell, if she didn't confess soon he felt compelled to hold her captive.

Would they be shocked to see their words published verbatim? He laughed. His stride was cocky, his steps certain. It was all going to fall right into his hands. He could almost feel the tickle in his palms.

CHAPTER FORTY-TWO

Zach took another sip of his coffee. It was cold, bitter and slid down his throat like a steel saber.

George didn't say a word, just studied his hands.

"George, I want you to know that I appreciate your honesty. I'm willing to work with you."

George nodded, his head down.

"This is a personality disorder. Can you tell me...whose name, or identity...?" Zach broke off, fearing the worst.

George stifled a sob, and then shook his head no. He began to cry, placing his head in his hands.

"Let's get out of here." Zach grabbed for the check.

George slammed his hand down over the ticket.

"You're not paying for this." He wiped his nose.

"All right." Zach put a couple of dollars on the table. "I'll leave the tip. Listen, we can discuss this at my office, your hotel, wherever."

George pulled some money out of his wallet and set it on the bill. "I'm okay. Let's just get this out of the way." He stopped and swallowed. "Joanne...Marquel." His nose started running again. He looked Zach in the eye, his tortured hazel eyes watering. "Marquel was our daughter. She's dead...I blamed Joanne at the time, but it was just an accident. A terrible accident."

Zach's throat closed.

George groped with his explanation. "Joanne, she loved her... we both loved her, maybe too much. I guess she just snapped..."

He looked out the window into the distance. "After the funeral, I called her…a murderer. A killer. That was my child they buried, she was my child too!"

He put his sunglasses on. He had worn them so much that first year to hide the pain, the hurt.

"I didn't mean it. God, you don't know what it's like to lose your only child…it was so brutal." He inhaled, then glanced out the window again. His lips twitched. He bit at his upper lip to control the nervous reaction. He wanted to get the hell out of there. He didn't even want to see Joanne now; it was too painful. "Joanne's a brunette. Never wore much makeup. She's pretty without it…" He calmed himself, shaking his head. "She's got Marquel's blond hair now. We always teased that we didn't know where our baby got her white hair. There are lots of kids with blonde hair and blue eyes when they're young, I know… We wanted to believe everything about Marquel was special. We agonized over what to name her. We never even considered that we might have a boy. We planned for a little girl." His sunglasses slid down his nose and he pushed them back up. "We narrowed the choices down to Quinn, Taylor or Kennedy. But Joanne converted the name Raquel to Marquel—that was it. Marquel would be our daughter's name." He looked at Zach again, finally. "Do you have any children?"

"A daughter."

George nodded. He didn't feel up to saying much more. He was calm now. Zach could tell him to leave and he would go without a word. Maybe Joanne had lost her mind. Maybe she didn't care. He loved her and he always would.

The hurt of losing his daughter and Joanne disappearing, compounded by his own guilt…It had to have taken years off his life—to reopen these wounds could destroy him. If only he could forget, like she had. If only he could escape the awful reality.

CHAPTER FORTY-THREE

Joyce boarded the L10-11 bound for New York City.

She'd been suspended from the show for an indefinite period and she didn't give a shit. She could find work on the stage. It was her first love. And there wasn't a producer, actor or stage manager that she didn't know off Broadway.

She would eat, drink and do a film here and there before inevitably going back to LA. But for now, she was going to cleanse her system. Go back to the smell of the greasepaint, the roar of the crowd.

That was working, *living*.

She took her seat in first class, eyeing the man by the window. "Mind trading places?"

She leaned in to give him a shot of cleavage.

"Not at all."

"Thanks." She brushed against him as they exchanged places. "Going east?"

"Boston."

"Great town."

"And you?"

"The Big Apple. I used to think, after moving to LA, I'd be lucky if I ever made it back again. But, at last, I'm goin' home."

"Good for you." He returned to his business papers.

She buckled in and adjusted her seat back, closing her eyes. She was nervous about seeing old friends again. Would they remember her? Would they care? She hoped *someone* still lived there.

The plane lifted off and began its upward climb. She glanced over at the gentleman who was seated beside her. He was gone. That was odd. She must have dozed off for a little while.

She looked to the rear and the stewardess gave her a nod—everyone was buckled in for the moment. The seatbelt sign remained on. Turbulence jerked the plane suddenly. Joyce looked out and could see the weather was overcast, but there was no rain or lightning. They were no longer climbing.

She glanced around again at the sea of faces behind her. They were descending, rapidly.

Everyone was screaming. What the hell was happening? She heard a crack, like a tree snapping in half, and she closed her eyes, screaming along with the others. Then she looked over. The row of seats across from her had vanished.

She collapsed against her seat, the atmosphere wracking her body and pressing her further into the seat. In the blackness of it all, the downward spiral, she sensed the impact of her limbs being pulled apart. But it didn't hurt. Somehow her brain functioned while her body stopped feeling.

It was okay. It was only the shell of the woman, the mold of her person.

She was free at last. Free…

The news carried extensive coverage of the plane crash that claimed the lives of all 221 passengers and crew members. Marquel collapsed in the hallway. She had wanted to throw up, but passed out in the kitchen where she'd turned on Lawanda's portable television.

Zach found her there. Both he and George tended to her, carrying her up to the bedroom. Zach tried to get her to talk, but could only make out her mutterings that, "Joyce is dead."

He'd heard about the crash on the radio. And now he had George there…

He wanted to give them a chance, but he didn't know how this tragedy was going to affect her. Just a few hours earlier, he'd had it all figured out—he'd be there for her, to work through it all with her. And George...Now she could suffer another setback on top of it all.

When she finally awoke, she found Zach sitting beside her, stroking her hair.

It was just becoming light outside and she realized something was wrong. How did she get up here? Why was she still dressed? Zach wasn't sleeping next to her, he was sitting in a chair. She had no idea that there was a man downstairs waiting to see her—and couldn't remember the news—the tragedy that caused her collapse.

Zach faced her, the whites of his eyes a painful red. She saw the obvious concern in his expression and it all came rushing back. Joyce...

Joyce was dead.

"How are you feeling?" Zach squeezed her hand.

"Zach, I can't believe it."

He nodded. He knew now why death frightened her. It was an unwelcomed monster that took life, never giving any reason, just leaving loved ones behind to anguish, to suffer the loss and torment alone.

"I can't go to her funeral, Zach. I don't know why...I just can't."

"You don't have to."

"I'm not well, Zach. My heart feels weak. Am I well?"

"Honey, this is all very rough on your emotions. You're only as healthy as you feel. But you'll get stronger once the grieving process is over."

He was on automatic now, rambling his textbook knowledge. "You may feel like sleeping a lot. Your appetite will probably diminish, but it all comes back. You just have to give yourself time." He wondered if she had grieved the last time over her daughter. Or did she block it all out almost immediately, to pretend nothing had happened?

It was all obvious to him now. Though he'd never had a case like hers before, he knew those who had suffered a psychogenic fugue took on a new life or identity without recollection of the past. He wondered if hers would be the extreme. In such cases, the fugue ends and there is no memory of the new identity, only the past.

George could trigger this in her and she may remember herself as Joanne Jennings, without ever acknowledging her life as Marquel.

"Zach..." Her eyes brimmed with fresh tears. Mascara stained her lower lids, giving her a painfully scarred look. She swallowed, then tried to tell him, but broke down again. Her shoulders wracked violently as she sobbed.

Zach reached over to stroke her back, but stopped.

What right did he have loving her? He wanted to hold her, but her husband—a man she couldn't remember—was downstairs, awaiting the opportunity to be with her. To love her.

"I'll give you a sedative. It'll relax you."

"I'm going crazy!" She grabbed his arm. "Zach, who am I...I'm mourning a woman I hardly knew and the thought of dying...Why should I be here, anywhere, if I haven't anything to live for?"

He was hurt, and he didn't bother to hide it. He knew she loved him, yet love couldn't save her sanity. If it could, she would have been well by now.

She reached out to him, hugging him. "You know I love you. But I don't have strength enough for..." She grew quiet. She wanted him to understand. "You're... you'll get over this. But I'm not strong enough to want to go on living. My mind is shattered—I should be institutionalized."

She was calm and trying to reassure him. He understood why she would believe he would *get over this*. Subconsciously she knew George's hurt. George blamed her and now she figured Zach's hurt would likely cause him to push away too.

It worried him. She was obviously asking for his help. Now he would have to decide what was best for her.

"You can go..." The reality of the situation hit him with maximum force. "God knows I've failed you. I've been so selfish."

"No." She tried to comfort him. "You've given me happiness...I'm just unable to reciprocate."

"I want you to rest. I'll give you a sedative and we'll talk later."

She knew there would be little to discuss, other than hospitalization. He wanted her to rest. And she was so tired anyway ... if this would help him to relax, she would take the medication.

After he'd given her the injection, he returned downstairs to George. The man sat quietly in the study. He appeared uncomfortable, as though he didn't want to touch anything.

"How's she doing?"

"I've given her something to help her sleep. The death of her co-star has made her deeply depressed."

"What do we do now?"

"I don't know if this is the right time, George."

George studied his hands. He knew it would come to this. How could he ever expect to see her when so many barriers stood in the way? How did he know the doctor didn't sedate her just to keep them apart? Perhaps Zach changed his mind.

The evening wore on, giving way to darkness. The phone calls began. Reporters wanted comments from Marquel. How did she feel about Joyce's death? Was it true they didn't get along?

Even Collins made the gesture and Zach gave him a pat, "No comment."

The two men sat by the pool, speechless. There was nothing to say, nothing to do but wait.

At three in the morning, Zach went to check on Marquel and found her huddled in a corner of the bedroom, crying. She said she didn't know why. Demons were haunting her; she wanted her mother.

"Marquel, I have someone here who might be able to help you."

She stared glassy-eyed at him. "Who?"

"Someone who knew you quite well. He can answer your questions. But first, I have to be certain you're up to this. Hospitalization might be needed, even once you have the answers. Can you do this now? Can you see him?"

She cried, "Yes. Dear God, yes, I need to know."

"First, I'll bring a tray up. You have to eat something and take a shower…I'll bring him up when you're ready."

"Who is he? A friend…family?"

"Both." Zach helped her to her feet.

"You're not going to tell me."

"You two will have plenty of time. Why don't you get cleaned up and I'll fix you some dinner?" He laid her clothes out—some jeans and a sweatshirt—then left for the kitchen.

"You can go up after she's eaten," Zach told George.

"I thought it wasn't a good idea."

"It probably isn't." He explained the dissociative disorder, psychogenic fugue, to George. "She may not remember you, still. She may not remember *me* if she comes out of the fugue. I'll help you both any way I can. She deserves to know…to meet you…again."

It was the least Zach could do for her. She came to him wanting to remember her past, and now he could give it to her. "It's going to be a shock, George, but she should begin to connect the events on her own, after you two talk. She has a right to know. She's suffered long enough."

"I don't understand. How has she suffered?"

"Goddamn it! Haven't you heard a word?" Zach slammed his fist on the counter. "She doesn't know who she is. She took on your daughter's, her daughter's identity to give her only child another chance. She didn't want her daughter to die. She sacrificed her life so Marquel could *live*."

"You mean…the acting thing, all of this is for Marquel?"

"Maybe it's what she wanted for her daughter. A fairy tale existence. Fame, wealth, a happy ending. But she can't carry it off. She's cracking. Somewhere within…Joanne is trying to get out."

George's head sagged. "We tried for so long to have a baby. The doctors said it wouldn't happen, but we never gave up. Then, after seven years, our little miracle came along…I had no idea a person could react this way."

"Joanne must have found the weight of her guilt and yours too much to bear."

George said nothing.

"We have to take this slowly. If I feel she's responding all right, you can tell her about the child. But for now, just explain who you are and give her a chance to digest it."

"Okay."

When she first laid eyes on the young man, she thought how very handsome he looked. He was dressed in a casual pullover and faded jeans. He appeared tired. Dark shadows pulled underneath his shining hazel eyes.

He approached her and took her hands in his. They were warm, rugged hands. Strong hands.

"I've missed you," he said.

She smiled, not certain how he meant it. "How do we know each other?"

"Well, first, we went to high school together. We were sweethearts."

"Did you know my family?"

"Your parents, like mine, had you rather late in life. When we met, you were living with your mother's sister. Your Aunt Irene."

"And my parents?"

He was so kind and soft-spoken.

"They both passed on sometime before we met. Your father died from a heart attack, and your mother, according to your aunt, of a broken heart."

"We were boyfriend and girlfriend?"

"Yes." He smiled. "You were hard to catch."

She felt suddenly shy, blushing as he continued.

He looked to Zach, who nodded, and he went on to explain that after high school they were married. She withdrew her hands from his. This stranger was telling her that they were once intimate. It seemed impossible.

"Do you want to know…?"

"I don't believe this. You're that George Jennings that Collins questioned me about. How do I know you're not being paid to say this?"

207

"Joanne, please."

She stared at him. "Why did you call me Joanne?"

"That's your name."

"That was my mother's name."

"Your mother's name was Helen and your father was Joseph Carter."

"He's lying, Zach."

"Honey, do you want to stop now?"

She was astounded.

"No," she laughed, a bitter sound. "Hell, *you* believed him. Let's hear it all."

George looked at the doctor, who stood there silent. He didn't seem to know what course to take.

"I think we should stop for now," Zach said finally.

"Stop?" Marquel turned to Zach. "Why? Give me one good reason."

"I don't have one."

"Then let George continue...I'm all ears."

George took a deep breath. "Your name is Joanne Jennings. We were married June 30..."

"Did you rehearse this?" She laughed again. "You're no actor."

"And you're no actress! You sit there, all high and mighty like you're some kind of innocent. Where did you get your name, *Marquel?*" he screamed. "Tell me, Goddammit!"

"What the hell are you getting at?"

"Don't you know, Joanne?"

"Stop calling me that."

"It's your birth name...unlike the name you stole."

"Zach, get him out!"

"No!" George objected and pled at the same time. "You want to know who and what you are? I'll tell you, sweetheart..."

She started to cry.

"You can't walk away from me now, not like you did, not from what happened..."

"George," Zach went to the man. "Sit. Let's take it slow."

"Slow? I've been dragging along at a snail's pace for the last two years. No. I'm getting this out in the open, here and now."

Marquel looked at Zach, her eyes pleading.

Zach didn't know what to do. But he couldn't bring himself to stop it... This wasn't the way he wanted it to go, but he couldn't stop George.

"Marquel was your daughter." George wrung his hands. "Our daughter. She's dead, Joanne. Dead. And you took her name, dyed your hair *her* color. You tried to live her life...but no more. By God, no more!"

He removed his wallet, throwing a snapshot on the bed, a picture of a platinum-haired toddler.

She picked it up. The child's angelic face, framed by bouncy curls, and the widest violet eyes tugged at her heart.

It was all flooding back now.

She looked at George, her vision blurred by tears. "Oh my God, what have I done?" She looked at Zach. "I'm so sorry."

Her heart beat heavily, the blood pounding in her ears. She could feel herself growing weak. She tried to get out of bed, but collapsed, into George's arms.

He caught her, held her, pressing his face into her hair.

CHAPTER FORTY-FOUR

The van was parked a block and a half away from the house. Within it, Collins and Dave were high-fiving each other.

"Joyce's tragedy and now Marquel...there is a God."

Collins shook Dave's hand. Hell, he almost kissed him.

"I told you this would pay off. Big. I didn't count on the Oswald plane crash, but it couldn't have happened at a better time." Collins typed on his portable computer, keeping his ears perked to the conversation in the house. It was all on tape, but he couldn't help wanting to hear it live. "I'm sending this in tonight."

"Then we'd better get back."

"Get this, Page One: Marquel's Secret Past—I Killed My Daughter."

"Whoa. Can you say that?"

"Didn't they?"

"Did they?"

"Would I lie?" Collins laughed. "Come on, I'm buying dinner."

"You're on."

They climbed out of the van. A note attached to the windshield explained that the van had broken down and somebody would be along to tow it. They climbed in Dave's IROC-Z and sped off.

CHAPTER FORTY-FIVE

Zach gave Joanne another sedative.

Neither man knew how she would react once she came around. They were both exhausted, having spent forty-eight hours without rest thus far. They agreed to take turns sitting with her while the other got some sleep.

"George, I don't know what you expect to happen from here, but she's on the verge of a breakdown. Hell, she's already having one. She may not feel she can trust either of us."

"Why wouldn't she trust me? I've kept nothing from her..." George didn't understand. "I wouldn't have come here if I didn't love her. She'll realize that...I know we didn't exactly do this right, but I know Joanne. We've had words before, but I've never stopped loving her."

Zach was exhausted. "It's been two years, George. Two lonely years."

"Lonely? You don't know lonely. I lost my little girl *and* my wife. You have no idea what two years of loneliness is. Look at her. She had no idea until now. She made herself a friggin' fortune. Sure, she was lost, maybe grieving in her own way. But I don't see where you get off talking about loneliness."

"I'm sorry," Zach said. He suspected he would find out about loneliness very soon. "Let's give her some time. We'll see how she progresses. I know this has been rough on you, but she can't pick up her past in one day."

"I'll sit with her. You sleep." George extended his hand. Zach shook it. "You've taken good care of her."

"I'll be across the hall. Don't worry about the phones. I'll have my service pick up. I've already cancelled the help for the next few days. I don't believe we need any added confusion."

"Get some sleep. I'll let you know if anything happens." George left Zach standing in the hallway. He walked into her bedroom and pulled the door closed.

CHAPTER FORTY-SIX

"Come on, honey, get in the car. We're going to the post office, then we're going to surprise Daddy."

The Dodge wagon had wood grain side panels and was at least ten years old, but George kept it in tip-top shape. They bought it the first year of their marriage, and now with a three-year-old, it seemed the family car was truly getting some use.

Joanne wore her favorite shirt, a pink floral print, and Wrangler jeans. Her long, brunette hair was braided in a ponytail down her back.

Her daughter, who had a stubborn streak a mile wide, wore her favorite yellow taffeta Sunday dress and a big yellow bow in her blonde curls.

"Can I get some gum, Mommy?"

"If Daddy says it's okay."

"Okay."

Joanne opened the front door of the station wagon and Marquel crawled across the seat. Swinging her legs over the vinyl front seat, she proceeded on to the back of the wagon.

"Oh no, we discussed this before. You have to sit in a regular seat, with your seat belt on." Joanne looked in the rearview mirror. The little girl had placed her hands over her ears. "I know you can hear me."

"No."

"Marquel, Mommy wants you safe. Besides, the policeman says it's the law. You know that. Now come on, get buckled in."

"Mommy, I be good. I sit right here and be still. Please?"

Joanne didn't bother to start the car. Her child had a mind of her own and it would take some time to get her to cooperate. She didn't have the heart to spank her. She only hoped the child would be this strong when she grew up and went out into the real world.

She watched her chatter quietly, laughing to herself.

She and George had been patient waiting for God to answer their prayers. The doctors said there would be no others after Marquel. No brothers or sisters, but they had their special little girl. What more could they ask for?

"This one time," Joanne gave in, "but only to the post office. Then you have to get buckled in."

"Okay."

Joanne buckled herself in. They drove down the narrow gravel road, shells crunching under their tires. Marquel sang her A-B-C's as Joanne glanced in the rearview mirror to watch. Few cars traveled down this road—an occasional hunter or fisherman during season, or one of the residents who had a home on the wooded acreage that stretched four and a half miles west to the Gulf of Mexico.

When Joanne reached highway US 19, she stopped at the stop sign next to the Bob's General Sore.

"Mommy, I can patty cake on my knees."

Joanne glanced back at the child. "Very good."

She accelerated across the southbound stretch of the highway, toward the median. Just then she saw the large pick-up barreling down the paved stretch at a high rate of speed.

"Marquel, hold on."

She swerved to avoid it.

"MOMMEEE," Marquel screamed a high trill as the truck crashed into the rear of the wagon.

Joanne's body jerked forward and went limp and she could feel the heat rising in the car. People were screaming. Her door was opened and she collapsed outward, feeling someone fidget with the buckle. They were cursing, obviously scared.

"Baby..." Joanne muttered.

"She's trying to say something. Christ, has anyone called an ambulance? Has anyone checked the guy in the truck?" The man picked her up and laid her on the grassy stretch of median.

A lady came running out of the Bob's General Store. "Did you get the child?" She was hysterical, her round body waddling across the street. "The little girl, is she okay?"

"What'd you say?" The man was confused.

"The little girl. Did you get her out?" The woman started toward the car.

Joanne raised her head and tried to move but her back was poured into dry grass. She could hear the panic and then an explosion. There were more screams now, as hot shards of metal showered the median.

The clerk fell back in a screaming fit of shock. The man went for her, but in her hysteria, she slapped and punched him. "Where's the baby?" She cried.

The man's face was expressionless. He didn't know what to say.

"You let that baby die!" She was wailing now. "God forgive you, you let that precious child die!"

The next days were black. Joanne heard their voices, felt their hands squeezing hers, but she didn't hear the little voice or feel the soft, tender lips kiss her cheek. And when she did open her eyes, she saw him there. His face was stubbled with growth, his hair matted, clothes rumpled.

They met each other's gaze with tears of happiness.

"They said you'd be okay. I was so scared..." His head sunk to her breast.

"It's all right..." She felt the tears spilling across her temples. "It's..."

She sat up, felt the room spin, and was looking into his eyes. George's eyes.

"Where am I?" She was startled. Then she realized it was Zach's bedroom, but George was the only one there.

"Oh George…" she cried.

He got up from the chair and came to her.

"It was awful."

"You had a bad dream."

She shook her head. "I remember now. Oh God, I saw it all. How can you ever forgive me?"

"I love you, Joanne." He crushed her to him. "It's okay. We're together, we'll get through it." He combed his fingers through her hair. "We'll be…"

CHAPTER FORTY-SEVEN

Joanne looked in the mirror. The hair…the blonde, matted locks looked like a cheap wig. Her makeup, smeared and dried, was an ugly mask. She ran some water in the sink and began to scrub hard at her cheeks with a washcloth, as though she could peel off the first layer of skin to find the real Joanne beneath. How could she have lived such a flamboyant life? It was so foreign to anything she had ever done or believed in.

How could she have taken the name?

Zach had explained in his analysis to her that she had taken on Marquel's identity to keep the memory of her daughter alive. But no matter how he explained it, she had still lost two years of her life and robbed someone else of theirs, parading around as someone she wasn't.

Joyce, her co-star, was dead. And yet it didn't matter now. She didn't know the actress any better than she knew herself. And Zach—she loved him. But she wasn't certain that their love was strong enough to keep her here.

There was no way she could go on pretending to be this star, this blonde actress. She screamed. Pulling at her hair, she wished she could pull it out by the very dyed roots. "I hate you!" she shouted at her image. "You monster, you've ruined so many lives!" She hit the glass, shattering the mirror. Long, broken lines split her reflection in two.

She slid down the wall and sat on the floor. She had to leave. She couldn't face either one of them now. She was still married to George, whom she loved and now remembered all those years with him, struggling and wanting a family. And she had Zach, whom she openly loved as she had loved no other. He understood her and could help her through this.

But it wouldn't be fair to George, who had waited, and come for her.

The thought of killing herself was most plausible—an answer to her problems, a way out. But she had already escaped; she had hidden long enough. If anything, she would have to face them both. She needed to find her place in the world; learn to live with what happened and learn to cope.

Alone.

George came to see her later.

Kissing her hands, he whispered, "Joanne, I love you. I want you to come home. I know it'll be hard for you, but I'll be with you every step of the way."

She shook her head. Her lips twitched nervously. She didn't want to hurt him anymore, but she could find no easy way to tell him.

"Are you saying it's over? 'Cause I don't think we've given ourselves a fair chance. I've gotten over Marquel's death. The things I said at the funeral, I didn't mean them. Hell, I probably made you snap…it was a rotten thing to say. I never held you responsible."

"It's not important. I hold myself responsible. What I've done since is unacceptable. Zach told me you saw my picture on the magazine cover. I'm so sorry you had to find out like that."

"I'm not. I might have never found you. At first, I thought you'd gone to get away from me—the ugly things I said. I always thought I'd see you again. That we would be together. It hit me hard to see you…to find you on the cover of one of those tabloids…but I believe we're meant to get back together."

"George, I know it's been a long time, but I need to think. I do love you."

"Is it the doctor?"

"He's taken good care of me." She laced her fingers through his. "He helped me. If you're asking do I love him, yes, I do."

He withdrew his hand. "Then what are you saying?"

"I'm saying I need time alone. Not here, not Florida, just by myself. I'm not going to run anymore. I want to stay in touch until...well...until I've sorted..."

"Sorted out who it's going to be?"

"No."

"Joanne, I'm your husband. I won't stand in your way if you want a divorce, but God knows I can't go back and wonder anymore. Wonder where you are, what you're thinking."

"I understand." She looked away. George had been there for her, for so many years, assuring her the doctors were wrong, that they could have a baby. He was wonderful during the labor and delivery, never leaving her side. "Give me the next few days to think. I promise, I won't leave you hanging."

He didn't answer, just walked over to her and placed his hands on her shoulders, massaging them.

"George..."

"Shhh, I just want my wife to come home. No pressure."

She placed her right hand over his.

Joanne and George sat down with Zach in the kitchen.

They explained their understanding that Joanne would give herself a few days to decide whether she would return to Florida. But Zach could see she felt pressured. The whole scene was too civilized, too absurd for words. Here they were, three adults, one with serious emotional problems, and two others trying to force her into a decision.

"She can't take just a few days and decide. Mar...Joanne, I want you to see another doctor. You need an unbiased opinion."

"What, from a friend of yours?" George asked. "An opinion where she should live?"

"George," Joanne turned to him, "I'll need to see a doctor whether I'm here or back home."

"And you will," George said, "but not someone recommended to mediate between him and me."

"Zach didn't mean that."

"Of course I didn't, George. I'm a doctor."

"And I'm her husband. You've been playing doctor more than you've been trying to help her."

"That's unfair." Joanne stood. "I'm not picking favorites here."

"I didn't mean that." George went to her. "I just want a fair chance. I'm not a medical expert…hell, he holds the cards here."

Zach stood. "George, I won't stand in anybody's way. I'm here to help. And yes, I love her."

He retired to his study. It was getting ugly, as Zach feared it would. He called his service and checked for messages. He was shocked at the number of calls that had come for Marquel. He didn't know what to do in light of the last few days. He had phoned in some flowers to Joyce's funeral from them both, but didn't bother calling Ken, Sid, anyone…Christ, he didn't know what he was going to do.

He ran his fingers through his hair. His temples pounded. He would have to call Jackie later. God knew what her mother was up to. God only knew…

CHAPTER FORTY-EIGHT

Pursuit hit the streets with Marquel's alleged confession that she had killed her daughter.

Collins had since sold a news syndicate an update on her secret identity, using direct quotes from an unnamed source.

A barrage of reporters camped outside the Manning residence, waiting to get a quote from the doctor or his mysterious lover. It was even rumored her estranged husband was holding them both hostage.

Lawanda carried in the trades and *Pursuit*, along with the wire stories published in the LA papers. Zach read through quotes, not believing what he was seeing. The person would have had to have been in the room with them to know...

Joanne locked herself upstairs, refusing to see even Lawanda. She was embarrassed. The woman didn't know her. No one did.

Zach had gone crazy. He knew Collins had gotten his information from within the walls of his home. He first attacked George, accusing him of selling his own wife's story to get even. But George didn't know about the stories until Zach threw them at him.

Did Joanne know? George was worried. The world knew she was a fraud, could they believe she had killed little Marquel?

They agreed to wait, but the reporters were getting restless and brave. Some threw objects over the gates, doing anything to get their attention.

They had no choice but to tell her.

The transformation was frightening. She wasn't angry, upset or even hurt. She said the world had a right to know. She was numb, her emotions torn to shreds. She laughed about it. It couldn't get much worse.

Fearing she would attempt suicide, Zach and George vowed to stay by her, no matter the hour. Zach scoured the house from top to bottom, finding first the bug in his office and later the one in the bedroom. He flew into a rage, threatening to kill Collins and all the reporters just beyond the gate.

The calls never stopped.

His secretary wanted to know what to tell the reporters outside his office. She feared they would break in and steal his client files. Ken was livid. He didn't know what was happening. He tried calling Marquel, but couldn't get through. He told Terry to keep trying, and to give them the word that he was on his way over.

When Ken pulled up, no one would budge to let him in. The gate was blocked, and the media surrounded his car, pushing television cameras and microphones as close as they could.

He let his window down a crack. "Clear the way, I'm trying to get through."

"Is it true you just learned today of your client's identity?"

"Are you going to mediate between the husband and Dr. Manning?"

"Is it true the doctor and the actress are being held at gunpoint?"

Christ, he hadn't heard that one. Maybe he shouldn't go in. "No comment. Move your equipment or I'm driving over it." He wouldn't. He didn't need any more trouble, but it sounded convincing. He laid on his horn. "Can't you move that?" he shouted.

He rested his head on the steering wheel. "What am I going to do?"

He got out of the car, pushing and shoving through the sea of people. He hadn't noticed until then that there were *Suburban*

Life fans holding banners and wearing black arm bands. They were loyal to the star. They chanted as he continued to force his way through.

"We've lost Joyce. Please, Marquel, don't leave us too!"

"We love Marquel!"

"Release Marquel!"

Ken didn't know what to make of it. He made his way to the security camera at the gate and buzzed for Zach. It seemed like forever before he got a response. Zach agreed to allow him in, but warned the reporters were not allowed inside. The gate partially opened and Ken pushed through, along with the reporters, fans and anyone else nearby.

Zach called the Beverly Hills Police to control the crowd and expedite the intruders off the property. Ken made it safely, but the mob managed to rip his jacket irreparably. Cameras flashed at every window.

Lawanda, Zach and Ken closed every drape and locked every door until the house was sealed off. They could hear the sirens, the police making their way through the crowd. Zach opened the gate to the BHPD. Thirty people were apprehended on the grounds, and officers were posted at both ends of the house and outside the gates. It was advised that someone make a statement to the press, and soon.

Ken saw Joanne for only a moment. George left them alone. But Joanne could only apologize and cry, telling Ken how sorry she was.

He prepared a statement that he and Zach reviewed. It was simple and to the point. Marquel's real name is Joanne Jennings. She had lost a child in an automobile accident more than two years ago. She never tried to hide her past. George Jennings, her husband, wishes to reconcile with her; however, at this time Marquel is still distraught over the death of Joyce Oswald and has no further comment.

Not surprisingly, the press didn't buy it. They wanted to know more. Why did the husband want to reconcile now? Why not tell the truth about the kid's death? Marquel was a negligent mother who wanted out, away from hubby and family to pursue the Hollywood dream. The allegations went on.

That evening, Joanne agreed to leave with George. She had seen the evening news and could think of no way to end the chaos but to leave. The police assisted Lawanda out, believing she had to get food for the house. When she returned, Joanne rinsed the blonde out of her hair and wore the maid uniform out. Ken and George assisted her to a nearby car.

It had been a heartbreaking moment, saying goodbye to Zach. He kissed her, holding her for the longest time. They both cried.

"I'm always here, if you need me. Always."

"I love you," she whispered. "I wish it didn't have to be this way."

He put a finger to her lips. "No regrets. All I want is your happiness."

She cried, not knowing if she could ever feel happiness again.

They went to George's hotel, and then caught a flight to Florida.

Neither she nor George spoke. It had been a roller-coaster existence over the last week, but now the previous two years had come to a close.

Zach took a long pull of scotch.

Lawanda was asleep in the guest room. Tomorrow night she would go home. The world would know then that Marquel had left him. He was a shell of a man. He looked in the mirror. His eyes were bloodshot, his face dotted with salt and pepper stubble. He looked at least ten years older than he was.

Angry, he threw the empty glass into the fireplace. There was nothing for him now. He wanted to feel he had done the right thing—that Joanne was well. Yet there was no way to reassure himself. If only those goddamned stories hadn't been published, maybe she would've stayed and checked into a clinic.

The alcohol felt good in his system. His senses were deadened. He was as strong as he wanted to be, indestructible. He could put his fist through the wall and not feel a thing. He grabbed the poker from the fireplace and swung it around, breaking everything in sight. The release lifted the crushing weight of losing her, if only for a moment. He was never one to lose control. But he also thought he was never one to fail anyone as he had Joanne. The burden was something he would carry for the rest of his life.

CHAPTER FORTY-NINE

It was eerie seeing the small cottage again. Nothing appeared to have changed. Periwinkles grew wild along the gravel drive. The pines and cedars seemed somewhat taller and thicker, but that was all.

They walked along the planks of the wooden porch, slats creaking beneath their feet. One board whined a familiar cry. Her heart felt weak, as though beyond the door time stood still.

George unlocked the deadbolt and stepped in first.

The smell, the musty scent of leather and wool hit her, causing her eyes to sting with fresh tears. The house smelled the way it always had when it was locked up for a few days.

She looked around. He had changed nothing. The old leather couch sat along the north wall, under the framed antique mirror that had been her grandmother's. The small kitchen and dinette set covered the south wall, next to the fireplace. It had all been simple. It had been home.

George carried the suitcases down the hall that led to the small bedrooms. Joanne ran her hand along the back of the rocking chair, facing the television. It was cool beneath her fingertips.

He stood in the hall watching her. He ached to hold her, to welcome her home, but he could see that empty look in her eyes.

"Joanne."

She looked up abruptly and swallowed. She hadn't expected to see him just then.

"Would you like me to unpack for you?"

She stared at him. How could she tell him she didn't want to step one foot further? Her legs would collapse beneath her if she did. She shook her head.

"Please, come see the rest of the house." His tone was calm. "You might as well get it over with."

"I can't."

"We've come this far. It's a small step in comparison."

"George, don't."

He came and took her hand.

She stood frozen.

"I'm here with you. I won't let you go." He walked with her, guiding her. Her body trembled, and her palms were damp and clammy.

The door on the left was a small, pink bathroom. She glanced and looked away. He steered her into the master bedroom, a ten foot by ten foot space with a double bed covered in white chenille. An oak chest of drawers and a dresser were opposite the bed, and several family photos hung above them.

"Joanne." He turned her to face him. His eyes searched hers for some sign of hope. "We can make it work, just give us a chance." He tipped her chin up, leaning in to kiss her. She turned away.

It didn't feel right. She could see the hurt in his eyes, but she was unable to open up to him.

"I won't force myself on you. It's been a long time for me." He wrapped his arms around her and hugged her, his head against hers. His heart raced as he felt her reciprocate this affection, hugging him back.

He leaned in to capture her mouth, kissing her hungrily. They both lingered there, caught in an emotion that had been shelved too long, remembering a special time that had once been theirs.

Afterward neither of them spoke, but remained huddled together, wrapped in each other's arms.

"Let's finish this." He took her hand and guided her to the other small bedroom across the hall. It too had been left intact.

The small toddler bed with the Strawberry Shortcake comforter was still lopsided, the way Marquel had tried to make her bed. A changing table with toys lining each of the shelves, mostly stuffed animals, was just as before. The closet door was open, all her clothes hanging in a rainbow of cottons, knits and taffeta. Her baby doll, named Cara, sat on a small table set in the corner.

Joanne felt suffocated. Her whole body quaked as her jaw twitched. "Ohh…" She felt herself choke. She threw herself down beside the small bed, burying her face in the comforter. "My…baby. God…I want…to…die."

George went to her, touching her shoulder.

She couldn't see his tears, his pain, as she slapped furiously at him, pushing him away.

"Leave me alone…Go, damn it!"

As he walked out, she crawled over to the door and locked it. She would never come out. She wanted to die here, with the feel and the smell of her sweet baby around her. She sobbed uncontrollably, certain God would take her in her hour of need, ending her insanity, her despair. Her suffering.

She remained locked in the room for two days. Each time George tried to talk her out, she swore she would kill him and then herself. He hadn't bothered to tell anyone she was back. He was surprised the press hadn't found them yet.

He knew only one thing: he wasn't going to call Zach Manning. He would take care of his wife himself. She would be fine once she got this out of her system, once she came to grips with reality.

CHAPTER FIFTY

"Lou? It's Zach. I just want to see if things are set."

Lou laughed for a moment then whispered into the phone, "Bogotá."

"You're kidding?"

"Would Lou Bartalow kid about such a thing?"

"How?"

"How doesn't matter. Mark Collins is now a permanent fixture in the fine, but very dangerous city of Bogotá, Colombia."

"Doing what?"

"Writing."

"Writing?"

"He was made an offer he could not refuse."

"Who's he writing for?"

"I don't know, to be honest. He's probably taking dictation."

They both laughed.

"Thanks," Zach said. "I owe you."

"Why?"

"I had nowhere else to run. I just couldn't see that bastard getting away with…"

"…I know. Listen, any time I can be of help."

"Likewise."

"So, how is she? Have you heard?"

"No. And I'm hoping like hell it's because she's happy."

"It must be sad. To lose and child and your mind. You'll find another good woman, my friend."

"I have the only woman I need. My daughter. God help me if I ever fall in love again."

"When the time is right. You take care."

Lou hung up.

CHAPTER FIFTY-ONE

Every muscle in her body throbbed when she woke. She didn't know if she had the strength to move. She rolled her head to meet a small white rabbit, eye to eye.

She smiled. "Hi."

She looked up at the ceiling, feeling like a bug whose body, wings and feet had been smashed to the floor. Only her eyes, ears and mouth were still intact, still able to watch the world above her. The towering walls, the changing table, the bed, everything, from flat on her back.

The sun shone its early morning trickle of light through the sheer white curtains, brightening with intensity as she lay and watched the wall bathe in yellow light.

It was as if a rebirth had taken place. The spirit of her daughter had risen with the new morning, filling her with hope, love and the ability to go on. She cried tears of happiness, feeling the reality and strength of God rise within her, feeding her soul, cleansing her sins and nourishing the frail existence to which she had wilted. She pulled herself up on wobbling legs, her clothes sagging around her body.

She unlocked the door, unlocking the past, and opening it to her future. She could see from the hallway that George was asleep in the rocking chair. She went to him, kneeling beside him, kissing his hand.

"Joanne."

"Good morning."

He hugged her. "I was so worried I would lose you again."

Her heart ached at his words. She wanted to tell him about the miracle that took place this morning. But there was no way for her to say it aloud.

"George, I have hope."

He sighed, stroking her hair.

"I know what I must do now, what will make me happy."

He listened, just watching her and stroking the auburn strands.

"I must go."

"What?"

"The memories here are overwhelming. I want to remember Marquel as the happy little girl she was."

"Then we'll sell the place and move anywhere you want."

"I'm sorry for what I've put you through. God knows I'd never try to hurt you."

"Like you are now."

"George, I want a clean start."

"So do I. You're my best friend, Joanne, my only friend." His eyes welled up. "How can you do this. How can you tell me you don't love me?"

"I can't. I do love you. But this love is too painful. You can have other children, George. I wouldn't deprive you of that."

"There was only one child in my life, and only one woman. I don't want anyone else. We'll pack up and go. Now. Please... Joanne, don't look at me like this. You're tearing me apart."

"I don't...it's just..."

"That doctor. You're going back to him, aren't you?"

"I don't know what I'm going to do." She stood.

"Please, Joanne." He grabbed her hand. "Please, I'm asking you...begging you...don't leave me."

CHAPTER FIFTY-TWO

Joanne carried the groceries close to her, hugging the paper bags to her body. Walking down the cobble drive to the motel entrance, she felt a pang of pride. It had been two months since she had moved to the small mountain community in Georgia.

She nodded to the older couple rocking on the front porch swing. "Good afternoon," she smiled.

"Oh...afternoon Miss," the motel manager said.

"What'd she say?" the old woman in the gingham dress asked.

"She said 'good afternoon,'" the man shouted.

The old woman smiled, her apple cheeks pushed high and pink. She winked at the younger woman, patting her hand over her silver cap of hair, making certain she looked okay. The old man continued to stare out at the road, as he always did, deep in his own thoughts. Occasionally he'd raise a crooked brown finger, acknowledging a car or truck.

Joanne grabbed the screen door with her pinkie finger and went in. Her room was on the second floor, overlooking the Blue Ridge Mountains. She heard the screen door squeal and slam twice against the door frame as she mounted the rugged carpeted staircase. The old couple rarely moved from their spot until it was dinnertime or after dark.

It had been a peaceful yet lonesome existence. She joined a small church and prayed daily for those she loved. It helped her sort out her emotions. She wrote letters to both George and

Zach, letting them know she was all right and that she hadn't abandoned her feelings for either of them. It grew more apparent to her now that she could never return to Florida. She had conquered those precious memories of Marquel, keeping photos of George and their child to comfort her in her despair.

She tried watching reruns of *Suburban Life*, but could barely sit through the opening. At first she felt embarrassed. It wasn't anything like the programs she and George had once enjoyed. The acting didn't bother her as much as the character she portrayed. It all seemed so long ago now, acting on a sound stage, arguing with Joyce, being pursued by Collins. She missed the work, but was sure she would never have the courage to try again or deal with the Hollywood lifestyle.

She placed the bags on the counter in the kitchenette. The room was small but quaint with fresh flowers on the table and window sill. She thumbed through the mail. There was a letter from Zach.

Having put the groceries away, she stretched out on the daybed and tore the envelope open. It was her first letter from Zach. George wrote once a week, each letter shorter and more upsetting than the previous one. She wanted to comfort him somehow, but her words seemed only to make him bitter. She suggested he find someone to talk to, a professional, but he never acknowledged her suggestion.

Zach was getting along fine. His letter was cheesy, his words light and fun. He missed her, he said, extending an open invitation for whenever she felt the desire to drop in.

She wrote back to Zach that night, telling him of the kind people she had met in the mountain community. She didn't know if she would ever want to leave, but if he would consider it, she'd take a raincheck on his invitation.

Tomorrow was a big day; she was joining a quilting class at the women's guild. This would put both her mind and hands to work.

Jackie answered the buzzer. Her father had been at work in his study and left her to tend all calls. It was time for Lawanda to come and she figured the woman must have forgotten her card again. But when she heard the doorbell, she wished she had checked the intercom.

She looked through the peep hole, not recognizing the face. Opening the door slightly, she examined the woman. Her dark hair, blue shirtwaist cotton dress and white pumps, her...violet eyes.

"Marquel?"

She smiled. "Well, Joanne, actually," she blushed.

"Sorry." She stared at her for a moment, then reached out and hugged her. "Daddy's been so worried about you."

"Is he here?"

"Yeah, come in." Jackie stepped back, opening the door wide.

"Thank you." Joanne was tearful. She embraced the girl again. "I'm so glad you're here with him."

Jackie too began to cry. She knew the whole story, the tragedy. Her father had told her.

"I thought I heard someone."

They both looked up, dabbing at their eyes. Zach smiled warmly at them.

"My two favorite people." He put an arm around them both and led them in.

EPILOGUE

Jackie fidgeted with her flowers. She tried not to look at her father; she didn't want to cry. Her nose was starting to run.

They looked so beautiful, Joanne in her beige Chanel suit and her father in black Armani.

"You may kiss the bride," the pastor said.

They embraced for a long, tender kiss.

She wiped her eyes with the handkerchief Ken had handed her. "Thanks."

"Don't mention it, doll."

The weather was humid, sticky and thick in the morning haze. George carried his rifle pointed down toward the ground, its safety firmly in place. He hadn't slept much the night before; he found it harder than ever before to accept his loss, to be alone. Joanne's letters had been of little comfort, leaving him to experience a void he hadn't been experienced when he…when he didn't know what had happened to her. It was as if each epistle was a carrot held in front of him, only to be jerked away. And the last one said it all. She was going to marry the doctor in California.

Their divorce was final just weeks earlier, and she couldn't wait to tie the knot. She said she might even consider acting in the movies if they would have her. When she was missing, there had always been the chance that he would find her. He had found her, but now she was really gone, never to be his again. Never to be with him…

He stopped suddenly when he saw the large gopher turtle walking across the path, its shell painted bright red at the top of its hump.

George shook his head. It couldn't be. But it was… the same turtle. He and Marquel had painted the red slash on the shell. *His* little girl wanted everyone to know it was her turtle, and George explained to her that she could always find him by looking for the red spot on his shell. The turtle had grown twice its size since and the red had faded. But it was still very visible.

George pulled a twig from a nearby branch and chewed on it. He didn't know what to do. He was tempted to take the big guy back to the house. But like his little girl and his ex-wife, he couldn't control fate. Tossing the twig aside, he switched the safety off and pointed the rifle at the slow-moving reptile. So much had been taken from him. He held the turtle in his scope, its small scaly head in his sight… he felt his finger on the trigger. His arms trembled. He could easily blow its head off, killing the pain inside him, the memories…

He threw the rifle down. He could see her…Marquel. Her small hands swabbing a paintbrush over the turtle's shell.

"Jesus Christ." He backed into a cypress stump.

He bent down and grabbed the barrel of the gun. It was no good; he had to get out of there. It was driving him crazy. Everything around him reminded him of…

In his rage, he swung the rifle against a pine, the barrel in his palms. He could kill no more. Life was too precious for such brutality. He gave the rifle another hard whack, hoping to break it or at least damage the gun.

His legs flew out from under him and he flew backward. His brain hadn't yet made the connection. The sound. The blood pouring from his stomach, drenching his shirt and spraying on dried leaves. He reached out for anything to grab hold of, his arms flailing, and all he felt was the thud of his skull crashing against the cypress stump. His eyes flew open, blinded by the brilliance of white light…it was warm, welcoming him…calling to him from above…

ABOUT THE AUTHOR

Emily Skinner lives in Tampa Bay, Florida with her husband, Tom. In addition to writing, she also enjoys selling advertising, and working with their daughters, Marquel Skinner and Blair Skinner on their film and acting projects.

Sign up for email updates at:
www.emilyskinnerbooks.com

Follow Emily on:
www.facebook.com/emilyskinnerbooks
www.twitter.com/emilyauthor
www.instagram.com/emilyauthor
www.thefilmmom.blogspot.com/
www.goodreads.com/author/show/6982753.Emily_W_Skinner

Emily W. Skinner
PO Box 8590
Seminole, FL 33775-8590

OTHER WORKS BY EMILY W. SKINNER

Novels by Emily W. Skinner

Marquel

Marquel's Dilemma

Marquel's Redemption

Booktrailer:
Marquel book trailer on YouTube—
featuring actor Eric Roberts & Marquel Skinner
www.youtube.com/watch?v=6e6O7iYqeVQ

Young Adult Novels by E.W. Skinner

St. Blair: Children of the Night

St. Blair: Sybille's Reign

St Blair: The Diary of St. Blair

www.ingramcontent.com/pod-product-compliance
Lightning Source LLC
Chambersburg PA
CBHW020758250626
47155CB00003B/1139